CROSSED LINES

LANA SKY

Crossed Lines

Crossed Lines By Lana Sky

Cover Design by The Illustrated Author Designs
Interior Formatting by Charity Chimni

ISBN: 978-1-956608-00-7

ACKNOWLEDGMENTS

There are so many people to thank for helping make this book a reality. Firstly, thanks Rebecca and Keeva because without your encouragement I don't think I would have been brave enough to finish it. Thanks to Erica and Mickey for editing this book with their amazing insight. And a special thanks to Shamooda for your lovely cheerleading, and to Charity for being awesome.

This book deals with sensitive subject matter and sexual content not suitable for readers under 18.

ONE

*R*eunions suck when your adversary is too good-looking to truly hate. All I can do is sigh dejectedly as my fingers fly across the cracked screen of my cell phone, documenting my pity party with the most elegant prose I can come up with.

:(*I'm in trouble with a capital T.*

T for Thorny, my unwilling guardian.

The last time we met like this was inside a lawyer's office. *This* office to be exact, though another balding man mediated those negotiations—which is how he likes to refer to our current living situation.

Negotiations.

For this rodeo, I sit primly on a leather chair and sneak glances at him from across the table as Grandmama's last will and testament lies between us. The old biddy didn't have a hand in penning it herself—her writing was about as legible as chicken scratch.

Still, we give her the due reverence required—the final say in micromanaging our lives. To commemorate this momentous occasion, Thorny stares from the windows, his arms crossed, while I keep texting Tiff from underneath the table.

My life is over, I type.

She sends me a frowny face, the extent of her emotional support.

I don't text back.

"Is Mrs. Thorne joining us?" Mr. Lawyer asks Thorny who doesn't answer.

Elaine, his wife, isn't here yet—go figure. She probably got lost on the way. What did my father call her, his pretty little sister? *Ditzy.*

You'd have to be ditzy to marry a man like Thorny. He glowers at his wristwatch, counting the seconds down. In ten years, he hasn't changed much, whereas I've sprouted boobs, shot up a few feet, and grown out my good-girl bangs.

He just got older. Gruffer. Grumpier. Though maybe he's always been this way? After all, it's hard to discern much about a person when your only references are photographs and shitty childhood memories.

He certainly *looks* older, Thorny. In that annoying way some people might find attractive. The silver in his hair brings out the navy in his eyes, and his face is all stern symmetry and chiseled jawlines—so stereotypically handsome that I could kick something. I bet his students deemed him bangable, a true PILF.

"Do you have anything you want to say, Maryanne?" the lawyer asks me.

Do I? Not particularly. Still, the occasion calls for a declaration of some kind to give Thorny a taste of what he's in for.

"I go by Juniper Berry now," I announce while simultaneously powering my cell phone off. "*Just* Juniper Berry."

Thorny digs his nails into the armrests of his chair as Mr. Lawyer frowns and shuffles the paperwork in front of him. Every last detail of my life is scrawled on parchment for his perusal, and he mouths the name stamped on each one quietly to himself. M A R Y A N N E. "Juniper Berry?" he asks, looking up. "I'm assuming that's a nickname?"

I shrug. "Something like that. I'm planning on having it legally changed."

"Oh." Mr. Lawyer frowns. "Well, I'm sure—"

"Knock it off, Maryanne," Thorny scolds from his corner.

Oooh. Five seconds until my first lecture. That has to be a record, even for someone as ornery as he is. I file the score away for later—records are made to be broken, after all.

"Sign," Thorny tells me, nodding to a nearby pen. "We're going to be late."

For what? I'd ruin my rebellious allure by asking out loud though. So I fold my hands over my lap instead and meet his gaze directly. Poor Thorny. His jaw clenches in disapproval. It's like he's pretending to be my father already, convinced he has the upper hand.

"Mr. Bell?" I turn my attention to the lawyer and smile sweetly. "I think I'd like to hear the terms again."

"No." Thorny sits forward. "I don't think that's necessary—"

"Please?"

The lawyer looks at me and clears his throat. I know his type. Rules and regulations win every time.

"Um, well… It couldn't hurt to go over them just one last time, I suppose?" He casts Thorny a wary glance but soldiers on. "You will reside with your aunt and uncle, Ms. Mayweather, until you reach the age of eighteen—"

"In three months," I interject.

"Yes, well…" Mr. Lawyer shuffles his papers and clears his throat again. "Until that time, you will reside with your aunt and uncle—"

"Technically, he is my *step*-uncle. Through marriage. Elaine is my only blood relative in this equation."

And, legally speaking, she doesn't even have custody of me.

Thorny is my sole guardian by order of Grandmama. In her view, he made for the ideal candidate given his stable, local job—unlike Elaine who gallivanted all over the world at the whims of her editor. Not to mention the theory that Thorny, a stern professor, could knock some sense into me.

Drunk on authority, he grits his teeth, his eyes flashing in that dangerous way that always makes Elaine flush. At family events. At Grandmama's old, stupid parties.

Whenever Thorny would touch his throat and narrow his gaze, Elaine would flinch. Then she'd jump to whatever command he would dish her way like a good puppy.

"Step-uncle, I suppose," Mr. Lawyer continues. "You will reside with them until you come of age and finish your schooling, upon which you will receive your full inheritance—"

"Blood money," I correct. "Specified by Grandmama, a portion of which will go to Thorny and Elaine as payment for being shackled with me. That is, when they don't have me thrown into the psych ward. Did my uncle tell you all about my psycho-ness?" I tap my forehead. "Borderline personality disorder. According to my shrink, I'm unstable, a chronic liar, and prone to volatile interpersonal relationships—"

"That's enough, Maryanne!" Thorny slams his fist onto the table, rattling the scattered pages.

Oops. One slides off the table and onto my lap. Juliana Mayweather's last will and testament in all of its bitter, passive-aggressive glory.

"Can we go now?" I flick the will toward the lawyer, who eagerly tucks it into his neat stack. Those damn documents have ruled my life for over ten years. Can't let one go astray. I might have to make my own choices, and then where would we be? Smiling, I turn to Thorny. "Can we leave? Huh, *Daddy?*"

"That's it." Thorny snatches up his briefcase and stands. From this angle, the light glints off the blondish stubble streaking his chin and my stomach flips over. He couldn't even bother to shave before coming to claim me. How disgustingly rugged.

His students probably clutch their ovaries during every damn class.

"Are you really going to start this now?" he demands.

"What?" I flutter my eyelashes. "That's what you are, isn't it? My legal guardian—"

"Get your things and let's go." He storms from the room, pushing past the startled brunette standing in the doorway. The receptionist, I assume.

She blinks at the man marching down the hall and then shakes her head, turning to Mr. Lawyer. "There's a call for you, sir," she says.

Mr. Lawyer sighs and extends a weathered hand for me to shake. "Well, good luck, Ms. Mayweather. Welcome back to Thornton." He follows after Thorny, leaving me alone with his coveted stack of documents.

For the hell of it, I tuck the whole damn file under my arm before stooping for the suitcase I discarded in the corner. My surly pout can't be helped. This isn't quite how I pictured my reunion with Thorny and Elaine, my parents in the eyes of the law.

I always imagined more screaming and hysterics. Maybe a broken item or two I could throw for dramatic effect. Damn Thorny for always having to ruin my fun.

A stuffy, important author such as him doesn't have time for dramatics.

Like a good parental figure, he's already left the office, leaving me behind. Abandoned, I juggle my suitcase with one hand while keeping the file out of the lawyer's view and shimmy through the door as best I can.

Thorny is already storming toward a flashy sports car parked near the curb. A bright cherry red, it gleams amongst the dour vehicles of this seaside resort's conservative upper crust. Thorny stands out in much the same way: a shiny tombstone in a grim yet exclusive graveyard.

"Shouldn't we wait for Mommy?" I call as I step from the shadow of the law offices into the glare of the midafternoon sun.

He was an hour late to this session—of course—but Elaine isn't in the passenger's seat of his two-door. Neither is she skulking around any of the nearby buildings.

Rather than answer, Thorny fixes me with one of those disapproving glares he could probably patent as a universal symbol for the *unwilling guardian*. "Get in." He jerks his chin to the car and wrenches the drivers-side door open. "Now."

Pity. At least, this time, he came in person rather than have his accountant attend the meeting on his behalf. Though that man was a real hoot, easy to play with. I think I made him cry once.

But not old Thorny. He's a much tougher nut to crack.

Resigned, I stuff my file into the side pocket of my suitcase. Then I carry the load to the car by myself and heft it into the trunk. After slamming it closed, I take my time slinking around to the passenger's side. My fingers graze the glass as I observe the clouds painting the sky in a grim patchwork. One minute, it's sweltering, fitting for the end of spring, but the next, it's chilly and gray and boring.

Like James Winston Thorne.

Irritated, he raps on the glass, but I pretend not to hear as the sun returns. It's blindingly bright, and I use my hand to form a visor. *Oh, sunshine.* I thought I'd never see it again. A week in a psych ward can do that to a girl, make her desperate and melancholy. Or so my psychiatrist says.

It's why he prescribed me enough tranquilizers to fell a horse, with a daily dose of Prozac for good measure. Thorny's one condition for bringing me home was *no more of her nonsense.* I heard him shout as much from the conference room where he and my treatment team met to discuss my most recent "cry for attention," as he put it.

"We think a change of scenery would be good for Maryanne," dear Dr. Fuckface, my lead practitioner, said. "We're worried about her mental state."

Thorny merely scoffed. "The cuts weren't anywhere near her veins. She's playing you all for fools."

"Maryanne," he says now. An electric hum accompanies the feeling of glass sliding against my fingertips. He's rolled the window down—just far enough to snarl. "You have two seconds to get in the damn car."

One.

Two.

Three.

"Coming!" I reach for the handle just as the car engine revs to life. That's one thing about Thorny: he's not like the others. No. He has no tolerance for "nonsense."

He'll leave me behind in a heartbeat.

Again.

I take my time pulling the door open, even as he taps the gas pedal, warning he could take off at any minute. *Vroom. Vroooom. Vrrr…*

Just as the car begins to drift forward, I plop down onto the leather seat. Smirking, I let the door close on its own, but an alarm squeals when Thorny starts to drive. It's still open.

"Whoops." I make a show of yanking on the handle, closing the door fully. "I'm so used to being the unwanted baggage you shuffle around that I forgot what it feels like to sit inside of an actual car with you, *Daddy*."

He says nothing, scowling at the windshield.

The sun is hiding again, but the clouds have grown thicker. Darker. Rain could erupt at any second—the perfect metaphor for what I do to Thorny's figurative parade.

Pour. Pour. Pour on it.

"It seems like you and Elaine have done well for yourselves," I say to strike up small talk like a good daughter. The fancy car. All those vacations to Italy. The beautiful mansion in the hills.

They're spending their share of my inheritance before the check is even in the mail.

"So…" I bite my lip and kick my feet against the immaculate plastic mat beneath them. "Which prison are you sending me to now? Our Lady of Sorrow? Saint Mary's? Windsor?" I extend my hand and tick every school off one finger at a time. "Oh, that's right, Daddy. I've been expelled from them all."

Still nothing. He's determined to ignore me today, old Thorny. His eyes scour the road, and he's gripping the steering wheel like hell. God, he makes it *too* easy sometimes, because one trick never fails to break his stoic-ass façade.

Rebellion.

I force a sigh and reach over to flick the dials of the radio. He had it on already with the volume down low—some classical music channel spewing out Mozart. Within seconds, angry rock blares from the speakers instead.

"Enough." Thorny bats my hand away with one of his and turns the radio off altogether. "If we are going to do this, then you trust and believe that there will be ground rules—"

"So," I say over him while eyeing my pink nails. "Since I've been kicked out of every school on this side of the country, does that mean I get to go to *yours*?"

Walden Academy. The coveted, prestigious school for girls that Thorny has all but nailed himself on a cross to ensure I'm not accepted into. No matter which well-meaning nurse, headmistress, or lawyer broached the topic, Thorny would deny them with some terse, polite version of "over my dead body."

"Ground rules," he says, grating the words off his teeth. "You have one chance, Maryanne."

"Just one?" I parrot, cocking my eyebrow. "Usually, I'm given at least three strikes—"

"I'm not your Aunt Lily," he says, naming one of his three sisters. Throughout the years, he's bribed them all into taking me in, using the various states they live in as an excuse to send me to the furthest schools. California. New York. Anywhere away from Maine. "Or Caroline. Or Marcia. Or your grandmother. You so much as put a toe out of line and I'll rescind my guardianship in a heartbeat and make you a ward of the state."

So serious. He even looks it, glowering over the steering wheel, not taking his eyes from the road once. He has them all fooled, Thorny. They probably believe he took me in truly out of responsibility—and not for the massive payday waiting at the end of this rainbow.

"But, Daddy," I say softly, "if I'm a ward of the state, then you and Mommy can't collect off my inheritance like the poor, pathetic paupers you are."

"Enough!"

I'm thrown forward as the car stops short alongside a country road. We've left the town already.

"One million dollars," Thorny says, deadly soft. "That's how much we stand to gain from you. And if you think you're worth the hassle…" He laughs. "You've been in the psych ward for too damn long. The moment you pull one of your stunts, you're done."

A smattering of raindrops lands on the windshield, giving his little tirade a bit of dramatic flair. Ironic, considering that Thorny is so damn stiff that no actor alive could portray the right level of apathy. They'd need a surgically grafted scowl and years of hostile tension to pull it off.

"Stunts?" I ask innocently. "Like what?"

He grunts out a noise that could pass for a laugh. "You know what. Stealing cars. Setting fires. What got you expelled this time? Having sex in public? Anything for attention—"

"But what else am I supposed to do for fun?" I waggle my eyebrows in mock seriousness. "Besides, isn't it a little too early to jump to conclusions?" I start to fiddle with the strap of my seat belt. "Maybe we should turn around and inform Mr. Lawyer of this new development?"

The threat almost always works the first time. Aunt Lily flushed but bit her tongue, as did Caroline and Marcia. No one wants to be deemed a failure after five damn minutes.

I beam at Thorny, watching him from the corner of my eye. He's straight as a board, his jaw practically chiseled from tension.

"I could lead the way?" I pointedly tug on the door, pushing it open just a crack.

When he doesn't relent, I open the door wider and brace my foot against a patch of grass.

"Maryanne." Thorny's using his angry voice, reminding me how big he is, how much he exudes authority. Six feet of lanky, lean muscle packaged in a tailored gray suit. "Don't you *dare*—"

I lurch out of the car, giggling as my skirt flounces around me. It's not my fault; he said the magic word.

"Oh, darn, Daddy." I tilt my head up at the sky, leaving myself open to more falling raindrops. They splatter on my cheeks and my nose, dripping into my mouth when I speak. "Looks like we'll have to go back after all. And, gosh, how on Earth will we explain how I got so wet?"

When a car door slams, I instinctively skip a few steps to my right in case he's marching toward me. I glance at the car, however, and he's still seated. *My* door is the one he closed.

"1623 Hartford Lane," Thorny growls to me through the window. "If you don't show up within the hour, I'll assume that you made your choice and I'll have your things shipped right back to the hospital."

The car engine roars to life, and I only have enough sense to lunge halfheartedly for the door as he takes off, peeling down the road.

Damn! There was always a fine line to toe with Thorny.

He was never like the others, easy to irritate and oh-so-hard to please. Gritting my teeth, I stare after him as rain pelts me from overhead.

I could go back to Mr. Lawyer with some concocted sordid tale.

But then he might bring up the tiny matter of my file…

No. I narrow my gaze as that red car turns a corner before disappearing from sight. After only a few steps, I realize he's not coming back. Old, dried grass crunches under my loafers as I pick up speed, painfully aware of how the rain is steadily falling harder.

The first mailbox I pass marking a lone driveway reads *1600.*

Twenty-three more to go. Conveniently, that seems like a fitting number, less than a month when all is said and done.

Plenty of time to ensure that Thorny learns the same lesson he's spent years trying to teach me.

Attachments are for fools. Promises are meant to be broken…

And, despite how pretty they may sound, empty words mean nothing at all.

TWO

*1*623 is marked by a shitty metal placard nailed to a wooden post near yet another driveway, partially hidden by weeds and underbrush. This stretch of road is littered with them, abandoned beachfront properties owned by wealthy families with too much pride to sell them and too much debt to renovate. Overall, the township of Thornton is just an outpost for the rich, where what would be considered creepy and secluded anywhere else is simply called "rustic." All of Frick Island is like that: a terrifying scenic postcard come to life in the most boring of ways.

I miss LA. With its bright, fluorescent-yellow sun and all the cheery interiors of the psych wards I was shoved into periodically. My last two schools—Hollow Vale Academy and Whorton's School for Girls—weren't too bad, either. Even despite their "no tolerance for rule-breaking," which saw me expelled from each one after about a week.

Which, I can admit, is a record. The first step toward personal growth is accepting your flaws. My name is Maryanne and I excel at being FLAWED.

Maybe that's why Thorny is so pissed this time? I've burned all of my bridges, as my case manager liked to say.

"This is your last chance," she would stage-whisper during our meetings, as if the nasty truth shouldn't be spoken too loudly. "One more escapade like what happened at

Whorton's and you could be a ward of the state. Your family could wash their hands of you."

Which everyone seems to think would be the worst damn scenario.

It's because the Mayweathers—all two of them alive, counting me and Elaine—are so damn loving, you see. Not to mention that, without my last name, I'd have no claim to my inheritance at all. Grandmama was very clear about that fact.

And even Thorny, no matter how surly and pretentious he pretends to be, would rather put up with my nonsense than watch several million dollars go right down the drain.

My God, I've never known people to be so damn *loving*.

I've been in rainstorms more compassionate than all of them combined. This one comes down in torrential waves, gluing my clothes to my skin so that the vicious wind can't blow my skirt up at least. Talk about consideration. Even the thunder graciously keeps its distance until the moment I crest a hill and finally make out the vast expanse of property on the other side of it.

I fixate my gaze on the house first. Large and white, with marble columns supporting a Victorian-style frame, flanked by a private beach. Déjà vu transports me years into the past. Coincidentally, it was raining back then too, making this wild stretch of private property seem even more foreign and forgotten to my childlike eyes.

"Damn." I exhale, impressed despite myself.

This is Thornfield.

Thorny *really* brought me home this time.

The sky above me shifts, allowing a stray ray of sun to pierce the cloud cover and ignite each raindrop. Bit by bit, the storm lets up as I keep picking my way down the paved road slicing clean through the property.

Much like Thorny, it's organized into neat, color-coded sections. Emerald, overgrown lawns. Tan, dusty sand sprinkled along the edges. Crisp, white wood marking the house and its surrounding structures. I used to imagine it as some giant dollhouse built by an overbearing artist who meticulously planned out the lives of his precious dollies.

But halfway through its construction, he got drunk and skewed the seemingly perfect eaves so that every finalized detail seemed slightly…off.

Elaine and Thorny sure have let the house go. The closer I come, the more cracks in the façade I spot. Finding them all becomes a game of neglected-estate Bingo.

The white paint has turned gray in places, revealing glimpses of the old wood underneath. Some stones in the driveway twist underfoot, uprooted by a thatch of weeds.

Tsk, tsk. Grandmama would roll in her grave. She entrusted this property to him and Elaine, after all. I guess I shouldn't feel so special: I'm not the only gift Thorny didn't want from her.

At the end of the driveway is the cherry-red sports car, its headlights flashing. Its tires spit mud as it comes down the road, just enough to illuminate me in a yellowish glow. Suddenly, the car reverses. Parks. Hunched over and shielding his head with one hand, Thorny climbs out and walks away, entering the house.

I feel a strange sensation tickle my throat. Did he get cold feet? As I draw even with the house's main entrance, I notice a pink suitcase tucked beneath the wraparound porch, out of the still-falling rain.

What a gentleman.

Hissing, I snatch it up by the handle and take the front steps two at a time. Something in my chest twists as I reach for the handle of a pair of oak doors. They could be locked. One nudge proves they aren't, however.

Surprise, surprise.

Thorny always did love mind games. A sick sense of black humor was the magic ingredient that made his books so damn successful once upon a time. Literary experts and critics alike were allowed to point out what I can't: he enjoys toying with people more than I do.

He's not lurking in the foyer to gloat—a treat I wouldn't be able to resist. The house feels…empty.

My footsteps echo as I drag my suitcase inside and dump it right in the foyer. At a glance, I don't find Thorny or Elaine descending the winding oak staircase or peeking around one of the two archways branching off the main entryway.

Excluding the pitter-patter of rain, it's *quiet*—that mythical ideal that didn't exist in LA, New York, or the other metropolitan cities I've been bounced around for half my life.

I can hear myself breathing, fast and shallowly. Panting. I'm tracking water and mud up the fancy staircase to an immaculate upper level. Contrary to the home's outward appearance, someone sure has gone all out in ensuring that the decorating scheme lives up to Grandmama's standards. Elaine, I suspect.

My, my, she does love white. It's the color of the walls. The drapes. The ornate doors with golden knobs. I remember being here as a child, but it doesn't look so grand in my memory.

Mainly because of Thorny. Surly and stern-faced, he barely let me out of his sight while Elaine sniffled and sobbed with the rest of the guests. Having the funeral here was another one of Grandmama's non-suggestion *suggestions*. Her uptown flat was far too small, and well, my father's home was out of the question.

Yellow crime scene tape doesn't go well with black, you see.

I swear Elaine decorated this place differently back then. In fact, I vaguely recall more...color. Only the shadows hold any now. They stain the walls like bruises, shifting at the whims of the abusive sun.

Thorny and Elaine have the room with the best view, I bet. The one overlooking the ocean: a metaphor for how their perfect lives look over the rest of us peons. Taking a guess as to where it might be, I head toward the south of the house, peering into each room I pass.

The master craftsman of this dollhouse ensured that every space has the same crisp, neat vibe. Like Elaine, with bedsheets resembling her white-blond hair and canopies every bit as flowing as those designer dresses she likes to wear. Fragile. Shallow. Unoriginal.

They all look the same.

Even the one near the end of the hall—far from hers with Thorny, I presume—with a yellow gift bag placed on the bed beside a card that reads *Welcome home, Maryanne!*

Oh, Elaine. How quaint. One could hope she won't wind up regretting those words. Though who am I kidding?

She'll choke on them.

All in all, my room is bigger than the one I had at Whorton's. *Yippee.* The bed frame is tan wood, with one of those gossamer canopies draped over the top. My ivory bedsheets are speckled with tiny pink roses, and my wide bay windows overlook a view of swaying willow trees and a stretch of emerald lawn.

I trail my fingers along the glass and picture Elaine stressing over every detail from the thread count to the heavy cream drapes. God, I bet she picked out the monstrosity I find lurking inside the gift bag as well: a turquoise sweater. *Eww.* Underneath, I find a silver bracelet in a velvet box, sporting a lone charm in the shape of a seashell.

Welcome to Thornfield, her card conveys in elegant script. She signed it herself.

Thorny did not.

I don't find him skulking when I return to the hall. Just a few more doors down, I discover an enormous room I assume to be the master suite instead.

It's the only place with some real damn color. The bedsheets are navy, and the oak frame lacks a canopy. A row of windows reveals a view of the ocean that would make any spoiled brat green with envy, and a sliding glass door opens onto a wide balcony, allowing an up-close view. Seemingly close enough to dive into, the ocean laps at a sandy beach for miles in either direction.

No wonder Thorny hasn't gotten rid of the property yet. It's the best damn bribe Grandmama's money could buy.

I pull my cell phone from my pocket and snap a picture. A nighttime filter makes it look more menacing, darkening the sky and turning the water gray. I send it to Tiff.

Welcome to hell.

She responds with a grainy image of a plastic card that says **HALL PASS** in bold white letters. *Tell me about it. This is the new protocol because of you. Thanks.*

I send her a smiley face.

She doesn't text back.

Sighing, I move closer to the balcony's edge and lean over it. It overlooks a terrace connected to the first floor of the house. The entire foundation must be built against a cliff, because the lower level has an even broader view of the waves. It's like they dance right up to the edge of the house, bowing before the holy king of Thornfield.

Thorny.

His majesty frowns down at his watery subjects while drinking straight from a brown bottle. The sun highlights the silvery hints of gray in his hair, and my fingers twitch, aching to tug on a strand or two. Just for fun.

I must have made a sound, because he looks up at me. The more he assesses me, the more he drinks. And drinks. And drinks. Finally, he sets the bottle on the railing and turns away.

Even this close, I can't hold his attention for long. Did he think I'd really walk all this way? No. He *hoped* I wouldn't.

A muscle in my jaw strains. I'm frowning. But why? It's such a lovely day, with so many opportunities to start over fresh.

Forcing a smile, I call out, "I love my present, Daddy." I brandish the silver bracelet so that the charm noisily clangs.

He doesn't turn around. So I shake it harder.

"I said: I love my—" *Oops.* The bracelet slips from my grip and lands at his feet, dangerously close to the edge of the balcony.

I wait for him to retrieve it, like any good guardian would. Instead, he meets my gaze, his eyes as stormy as the clouds overhead. My stomach lurches, even before he shifts. I watch in slow motion as his foot nudges my bracelet, maybe by accident—maybe not. Either way, *poof.* It slips through the gaps in the banister and out of sight.

Damn. I smother a frown. Unlike the hideous sweater, I actually liked it. Though, rather than give Thorny the satisfaction, I blow him a kiss and wave.

He cocks his head as if picking up a sound I can't hear. In the same motion, his elbow nudges the bottle, sending it toppling over the railing. By accident?

I can't tell as he walks in my direction, presumably toward what caught his attention in the first place. Intrigued, I copy him, slipping back into the master bedroom. On my way to the door, I spot a dresser cluttered with the knickknacks of blissful married life. A woman's necklace. A crumpled navy tie. A discarded men's leather watch.

It's not stealing if it's a gift—and he owes me. I snatch the watch and tuck it into the pocket of my skirt. It's heavy in the damp fabric. I'm still soaked, and my shoes squelch with every step, leaving a noticeable trail of watery footprints.

Oops.

I follow them back into the hall and strain my ears to catch the faint hum of voices.

A man grumbles something surly and unintelligible. Thorny.

"What about dinner?" a woman replies, her soft, sweet voice tickling the air. "I thought…you would take her…reconnect."

Thorny grumbles some more, and I take the liberty of filling in the blanks. *She pulled her nonsense again. Why did we even take her in in the first place?*

"James," Elaine gently scolds. "We talked about this. It's only for a little while, and you promised: we were going to both try to make this feel like home for her."

They sound closer now. In the foyer, I assume. Tiptoeing toward the staircase, I can make out the golden silhouette of Elaine herself. Still blond. Still tan. Still fond of flowy satin dresses. The one she's wearing now is a light blue that contrasts with the curls spilling down her back. Dangling from one slim hand is a shopping bag. In the other, she's holding a bouquet of flowers.

Thorny faces her, his arms crossed. "I warned you," he says like the all-knowing paragon of wisdom he pretends to be. "You don't know that girl. She's—"

"Aunt Elaine, is that you?" I skip merrily toward the top of the stairs as if just catching the sound of her voice.

"Maryanne!" Elaine contorts her lipstick-coated mouth into a grin and advances toward me, her arms outstretched.

Over her shoulder, I meet Thorny's gaze and wink. He glowers, and my brain plays that dangerous game of guessing what he might have said. *She's damaged, darling. A nightmare, darling. She's beyond all damn hope.*

"Gosh!" Elaine stops short at the bottom of the staircase. "You look so much like..." She bites her lip to avoid mentioning that unmentionable person.

Your mother.

Clearing her throat, she eyes me again. "But you're wet! Did you two get caught in the rain?" She glances at Thorny only to wrinkle her nose at his immaculate appearance.

"I decided to walk," I say, shrugging. "Get some fresh air and take in all Thornfield has to offer. I haven't been here in ages."

I sneak another glance at Thorny, but he's turned away, his jaw twitching. I imagine him grinding his teeth, waiting for the moment my nonsense might come out in full force. When I'll prove him right.

"A walk?" Elaine sounds unconvinced. "You're absolutely flushed." The moment I descend the bottommost step, she lightly pinches my cheek. "You're about as ripe as a tomato."

"It's new blusher," I say, stepping out of her reach. "Sports-car red. I say it goes marvelously with my eyes, don't you think?"

Still facing away from me, Thorny doesn't give me a reaction to go off of.

"By the way, I loved the bracelet," I tell Elaine. "Truly, I did."

She blinks. "D-did?"

"It fell when I was admiring the view from the balcony," I say, shaking my head contritely. "It was gone in a flash. I mean, someone could have kicked it right beyond my reach, it went so fast—"

"I'll be in the study," Thorny says over me. He marches toward one of the archways.

"Maybe you could help me find it later, Dad—*Uncle* Thorny?" I call after him.

He hunches his shoulders.

Elaine giggles. "Oh, sweetheart, he hates going down to the beach. And 'Thorny'? I haven't heard that nickname in so long…" She trails off. "He prefers James though. And you don't have to call me Aunt Elaine. Ellie works just fine."

"Ellie," I parrot. "So, not Mommy?"

"What?" Elaine's pretty smile collapses around the edges.

Already through the archway, Thorny sighs.

"I'm just kidding," I say loudly enough for him to catch.

"Oh!" Elaine regains her flawless grin and all is well. "It's nice to see that someone around here has a sense of humor." She sneaks a glance over her shoulder as if to ensure that her husband is far out of earshot. "Anyway, has your uncle given you the full tour yet? The view from the Bluffs is unlike anything you've ever seen. Did you two go walking together?" She eyes my damp skirt again.

"Of course," I lie while running my fingers through my hair. The rain pounded it into a frizzy mess, and it's already straining against the confines of my headband. "In fact, I was just about to head back out and get some more fresh air."

The rain has let up, it looks like. The sun is sneaking through gaps in the white drapes, taunting me. It's like Thorny in a way: there in theory but gone the moment I open the door and step out to meet it. *Poof.* The clouds return, having one last laugh at my expense.

"Are you sure?" Elaine wonders as I descend the front steps. "It looks like it might rain again…"

"Don't worry," I call back. "James told me that the only true way to experience Thornfield is right in the middle of a big-ass brewing storm."

I can't resist glancing back to see her reaction. Faint-pink colors her cheeks, tainting the thick layer of makeup rendering her skin pore-less.

She chuckles in that halting, unsure way most adults tend to: helplessly. "Well… Just try to get back soon. I'm going to make dinner in your honor, okay?"

I turn, rolling my eyes. "Wonderful!"

For all of my bravado, it does look like it's going to rain again. Thunder rumbles ominously, growling above the faint hiss of crashing waves like nature's game of cat and mouse. Dark-purple clouds swell overhead, resembling the fat blueberries that grew on Grandmama's property. I used to pop them between my fingers, watching them explode and coat my hands in purplish guts. The scraggly, overgrown trees on the edge of Thornfield look sharp enough to puncture one of these storm clouds.

Plop.

I can already feel the cool drops splattering my forehead again. Flash. Lightning sparkles in the distance like gaudy glitter and my steps falter. Looking back, I can see Elaine still standing on the porch, watching.

Oh, Elaine. She always was the worrywart of the two. The one who pretended to care and nurture while heeding her husband's every word. If Thorny told her to jump, she'd skip to the edge of the balcony and sheepishly inquire as to how high.

Then he'd scoff and tell her to forget it. His only goal was to test the strength of his leash anyway.

For all of her gift bags and smiling bullshit, I know who really is responsible for my coming here. Thorny must be playing a mind game at my expense. Oh, I know: Elaine probably bugged him for children. She is thirty-five, after all, and her baby clock is ticking. "Sure," Thorny probably said, "Have your children. As many as you want. Just deal with this one first."

I'm the pressure subtly applied to make Elaine cry "uncle." Then he'll get his way, like always. It's what I would do.

Old Thorny may not be related to me by blood, but we think the same way. A lack of empathy, as one of my therapists put it. We're cruel and callous, and we don't give a fuck about anyone but ourselves.

It's the money that makes us this way. So damn much of it and all the freedom it implies, but with no way to touch a cent. We're shackled to the whims of Grandmama, even from the grave.

I'm tolerated by a family too proud to make me a ward of the state, and Thorny is too stubborn to relinquish his grip on this crumbling estate. He'd rather watch it rot. Like how the overgrown underbrush nibbles at the cracked roads, creeping over faded picket fences. The cloud cover paints everything in shades of silver and gray. The earth is withering just like Thorny's hairline. He may drive through this place in his fancy sports car, but the garage is just a few years from collapsing altogether.

I think my therapist would name his mind state denial. A house, you see, is a lot like an unwanted child under one's guardianship. Fancy legal documents may say it's yours, but at the end of the day, that level of power just gives you license to watch it collapse underneath its own weight and call it mercy.

It should be grateful. You kept it in the family at least.

One thing about Thornfield stands out from my hazy old memories. With only a vague sense of direction, I creep along the field until I find a path between two bowed trees, marked with a few stones hammered into the ground.

Once upon a time, my uncle Thorny took me this way, his big hand in mine. I can see him as clearly now as I did back then: so tall that he blotted out the sky peeking through a canopy of green. His hair had been blonder, his posture bolder. "This way," he told me. "You can't get into trouble in this place. Stay here."

In the real world, my fingers brush the ragged surface of tree bark and I'm back in the present, standing before the same destination Thorny brought me to all those years ago. The old oak is still standing, with a misshapen tree house tucked within its branches. Square and cramped, it looked old back then and appears even older now.

I lift my foot and test the bottom rung of the wooden planks nailed to the base of the trunk in a makeshift ladder. The first one still holds, and I strain on tiptoe to grab the highest point I can reach. Gradually, I make it all the way to the top, and only one plank feels loose enough to skip entirely.

Entering the tree house proper is a little trickier. I have to balance myself against a thick branch and shimmy through the crude opening, blocked by a stained piece of plastic sheeting.

Lord only knows who built this thing in the first place. Thorny? For all of those boys he'd never have. A secret place they could conspire away from Elaine—before he turned it into a prison for a bratty girl during her father's funeral.

It feels just as cramped and confined now as it did back then. The wood is stained and warped in places, and the floor is covered in leaves that rustle ominously the farther I crawl inside. Only snippets of light reach in through gaps in the planks, painting stripes over the shadows.

Thorny took me here, guiding me up those planks, and told me to stay put. So I did, like a good little girl.

Until I couldn't.

When I picture him, it's always how he was that day. In that moment when I stormed into Thornfield Manor's gilded drawing room, trailing dirt and mud. That cold, heartless expression when he realized I'd disobeyed. The way his eyebrows knit together when I did what I did next.

I made a scene.

He sent me away.

So, now, we're even Stevens.

Was it really the Whorton's incident that made him cave after so long? I mull over the prospect while clearing a space on the floor with my foot and curling up in that tiny corner. Maybe that scandal was one too many?

Even I can admit that it got a little out of hand.

But Thorny is Thorny. There has to be more to it than that. He brought me home after so damn long. Maybe it's to punish me…

Like a real daddy.

I laugh, but it rings hollow. Annoyed, I say out loud, "Fuck Thorny." He doesn't scare me. *Oh, no siree.*

In fact, he doesn't even deserve the same reprieve I extended to Caroline, Marcia, and Lily. I gave them a week of good, sweet Mary. That fun creation crafted from giggles and lies, who shits sparkles.

Thorny would see right through her anyway. No, sitting here, in a shitty excuse for a house, I'm convinced that it's better to just cut to the chase. I'll give him a day before putting my plan into action.

Thorny will cry "uncle"—figuratively, anyway. That is if he doesn't ship me off first thing tomorrow. I shouldn't care if he does. A house is just a house, after all. It doesn't matter if it's *the* house. The place where everything started like a series of falling dominoes.

I never wanted to live at Thornfield.

Not really.

I never wanted him to keep me.

Not really.

It never hurt that he didn't want either of those things.

It really didn't.

THREE

Elaine's fretting in the entryway when I step through the front door just as a new smattering of raindrops lashes at the eaves of the old house. Rickety Thornfield Manor sways in the wind, caught helplessly in the tempest. One good gust and the whole thing might blow away.

It's like the entire two-story structure is a literal metaphor for Elaine. Weak and pale, with patchy paint partially covering the glaring flaws. Skinny structures, draped in white and left to wait for Thorny to enter and exit as he pleases.

"Oh my God!" Her eyes widen, and she sinks to her knees, grabbing my arm. It's a patchwork of browns and purplish hues. "What happened? Did you fall? James!" She calls for him until he appears in the doorway, a wine glass in hand. "Look!" she exclaims. "Should we take her to the emergency room?"

Thorny takes one look at me and scoffs. "She's fine." He dips a finger into his wine and comes close enough to swipe the liquid over the deepest, darkest of my "bruises."

Like magic, they wash off, revealing pale, unblemished skin underneath.

I snatch my arm back, foiled again. "It's just a little dirt," I tell Elaine with a smile.

"Oh…" She frowns when I tap my muddied shoes against the polished floor but musters up a smile of her own once she catches me staring. "Well, I put your suitcase in your room. We can toss your things in the dryer if you need to." Her lips twitch. Guilt, I guess.

Difficulty with emotions is one of the many flaws my therapist lumped into a long, complicated diagnosis to explain my behavior: *Maryanne displays some symptoms of borderline personality disorder. She has difficulty recognizing and processing emotions.* Up is down and down is up to a freak like me. I struggle to interpret…oh how did he put it?

Compassion and love in a healthy way.

My broken brain is dangerously suspicious of both. Like how Elaine must be when Thorny takes that fancy new car of his out for a spin. Just who is he trying to impress?

Not her. Elaine is a rock, easy to please, with a few accessories glued onto her lifeless frame for funsies. You can pet her. Maybe love her. But it doesn't really matter in the end, does it?

It's not like she'll leave. The poor thing has no legs.

"I made dinner," Elaine says, clearing her throat as the storm picks up. "We can wait for you to wash up and change. Oh, and a friend of mine—*James's*—might stop by. I hope you don't mind?"

"Of course not." What's a good homecoming party if it's not hijacked by old acquaintances? Faking a smile, I take the stairs two at a time and then enter the room designated as mine. For now. I can almost see the inevitable expiration date stamped on the damn door as I pull it open.

Elaine left my suitcase by the bed. How sweet. She even folded her hideous sweater and left it there, too: my costume in their twisted family charade.

I should wear it. Make myself smile pretty while she and Thorny play happy families before I ruin everything and prove him right. I'm a broken screw-up. He's banking on that outcome.

That's why I don't even bother to unpack. Instead, I kick my suitcase open and snatch a dress from the haphazard mess thrown inside. The only thing I bother to treat with any care is my file containing its oh-so-precious documents. I scan the room for a good hiding place, eyeing the white dresser in the corner. No, too obvious. I cross over to the bed and shove the file beneath the mattress.

Across the hall from my room, I find a bathroom, where I shower. And shower. And shower.

Through the spray, I can hear angry footsteps stomping up the stairs. Heavy. Impatient. They march in my direction with purpose. *Thwack!* The bathroom door jumps as someone knocks just once.

"Maryanne."

The water is scalding. *It* makes my cheeks catch fire and ignites an inferno beneath my skin—not him. Even still… I'm hidden behind inches of wood and a plastic shower curtain, but I do that thing only he can make me do: bite my lower lip and think, just for a second.

I'm not used to hesitating—another quirk the therapists like to point out. *Hesitation is normal to help with impulse control, Maryanne. You should think through your actions.*

"It's been two hours," Thorny says. Like always, a sigh laces his words and he speaks to me in two languages. One is English. The other is nonverbal James Thorne: *Elaine made me check on you,* he grouses. *You're pushing it.* "Are you planning on joining us for dinner?"

I don't answer, still thinking. Two hours—has it really been that long? I inspect my pruned fingers and my shriveled toes. Then I pick up a damp washrag and scrub some more. *La-dee-da.* I pretend not to hear him sigh again.

"Ten minutes," he warns before stomping away.

The moment his footsteps fade, I switch the water off and climb out. Through a cloud of steam, I eye myself in the mirror, inspecting blurred, obscured limbs and a pale, blobby face.

I'm pretty, they say. Pretty like my mother before she got her nose job. Pretty like those boring girls placed beside the starlet in movies. Oh, so pretty.

Not *beautiful* like Elaine. Or any of Thorny's three sisters.

Poor self-esteem is why I overcompensate with sparkling clothing and outrageous headbands. My style is calculated to draw the max amount of attention and drama. I'm incapable of confining to social norms; therefore, red sequins and six-inch heels make for the perfect dinnertime outfit, in my opinion.

Or something like that. I read it in a book.

I'm in the middle of brushing my hair when I hear the front door open downstairs and a man's voice call out.

"Elaine, you look stunning! And come here, you son of a bitch."

"Oh, Jeremy," Elaine simpers.

I groan out loud. Jeremy Weston. Thorny's literary agent once upon a time. Now, he's a famous author in his own right. He bragged as much at my father's funeral—and even Grandmama's.

I hate him.

But the more the merrier. I leave my room noisily, balanced on my impossibly high heels, and follow the sound of meaningless chitchat to the back of the house.

"Maryanne." Elaine humors my outfit with a forced grin when I finally make my way into the elegant dining room just off the main entryway.

Thorny scowls. He's holding a glass of wine, keeping the bottle closer to his place setting than Elaine is. At least three chairs separate them on the same side of the table.

Like a good daughter, I claim the one directly between them.

"Look who showed up," Jeremy says, giving me a wink. "It's a movie star."

Where Thorny aged with a stubborn grip on his good looks, Jeremy threw attractiveness to the wind. He's gained at least ten pounds. His dark hair has a glaring bald spot right over the center of his head, and a layer of cologne can't disguise the stench of old cigars.

"Long time, no see, Mary," he says. "You've certainly grown up."

He stares at my chest.

"That's an…interesting outfit, Maryanne," Elaine says politely.

I finger the neckline of my dress and shrug. "What? This old thing?"

Thorny says nothing. Out loud, anyway. His gaze gives me a slow, scathing perusal I feel down to my goddamn toes. My sparkly, scarlet evening gown doesn't draw his ire, or my wet, damp curls—he knows the truth. *Caught,* a part of me whispers as my stomach clenches in that naughty-girl way.

Gritting my teeth, I ignore it and reach for a glass of water Elaine already had waiting for me because she's fucking perfect. I down it. Then I smile.

"What's to eat?" I say it solely to prompt Elaine's prideful glance at the food steaming before us on three porcelain platters. I wonder if she had to reheat it while waiting for me. The corner of my mouth quirks. Of course she did.

"It's just a little something I whipped up to celebrate," she says, preening in her simple blouse and skirt. "Um, there's spaghetti with fresh basil. A tossed salad. And some cut fruit for dessert."

She worked so hard. I can practically taste her blood, sweat, and tears in the humid night air. With the rain having stopped, she and Thorny left the windows open, allowing in the breeze blowing off the ocean. How quaint.

"It all looks so lovely," I gush. "But..."

Thorny braces his hands on the table, inhaling sharply.

"I'm allergic to tomato sauce," I say, pointing to the spaghetti. "And fruit." My finger darts to the glass bowl of fresh strawberries and watermelon. "And I'm allergic to salad."

"Maryanne." Thorny didn't even put effort into huffing my name that time. He shoves his plate toward the center of the table and stands. "I'll be in the study."

"But it's dinner." Elaine struggles to hold on to her perfect smile. It quivers at the edges, clinging to her pink lipstick with all it's worth. When Thorny meets her gaze, her lips fall flat. "I-I could make something else?" She looks to me, her eyes wide, pleading for me to laugh. To confirm I was joking, haha. With one little gesture, I could salvage her charming meal.

"I have a long list of allergies," I say, but I don't look at her as I do.

Thorny's eyeing his wristwatch, shaking his head. *Tsk, tsk.* What a waste of time I am. Of space.

"And you know what?" I tell her. "I'm not really hungry, either."

"W-wait!" Poor Elaine stares on in horror as I skip past Thorny.

My work here is done. So pleased with myself am I that I don't see him move until it's too late.

"Oh no you don't."

My arm is in his grip. Like a leash, he uses the limb to drag me from the room, out of Elaine and Jeremy's line of sight.

"I've heard the horror stories," he hisses near my ear with far more vitriol than a good daddy should muster. "But my God. You really don't have any goddamn shame, do you?"

He lets me go in disgust. As his upper lip pulls back from his teeth, a part of me exclaims, *Aha!* There he is: the real Thorny I remember. The man with eyes like those stagnant pools of water left after a rainstorm. Dark, frothy things with plenty of unseen horrors lurking within.

"I don't know what you mean," I say softly, brushing my fingertips along my throat. "I really am allergic. One bite and I could *die.*"

He smiles ferally, which is something he excels at: making harmless gestures into insults. From him, a grin is a missile, loaded with double meaning.

"Tell me why I shouldn't ship you back to Los Angeles," he says, daring me again. "Give me a reason."

I blink, fluttering my eyelashes so hard that my view of him is sliced into snippets. I can track every nuance of his expression in stages like this. His jaw tenses, tenses. Boom, he's frowning and something makes me take a step back.

So he can see me better, the bane of his existence.

"One reason? Hmmm…" I tap my chin with my thumb. "How about: I'm *sorry*, Daddy?"

"You're not." He reaches out, snagging a fistful of my skirt. One tug yanks me closer to him. Close enough to breathe in the wine tainting his breath. "Lily told me she was missing clothing after you left," he says, eyeing me through a narrowed gaze. "Dresses. Shoes. Jewelry. You know—" His grip tightens, but I dig my heels into the floor to keep my balance. The harder I resist, the more he tugs, until I'm forced to take a hasty step toward him anyway. "You may be seventeen, but she could still press charges against you."

His eyes ignite with smugness. Poor Thorny. He doesn't even know what game we're playing. Rising onto tiptoe, I press my lips to his cheek. They barely make contact as he jerks out of my reach, letting me go.

"She won't," I tell him, confident of the fact. Smoothing my hands over my skirt, I cock my head thoughtfully. "But, even if she did, there are plenty of secrets about her and her husband I could spill in return. Wouldn't that be just marvelous?"

He watches me, his expression unchanged. There's no surly frown of defeat. No hint of curiosity. My stomach twists again and I grit my teeth. I hate this fucking feeling—not knowing what he's thinking.

"Good night, Daddy," I say. "Tell Mommy I'm sorry about dinner." I blow him a kiss and turn to make my exit. Even he has to admit it now: I have the upper hand.

"One month," he says, and my feet stop in their tracks.

Sneaking a glance back at him is too risky. My cheeks feel hot again. Inflamed.

"Hmm, Daddy?" I call over my shoulder.

"I bet you couldn't last one month without fucking up."

"You shouldn't make wagers without naming a price, Daddy," I tell him. Again, I start for the stairs.

"Our share of your inheritance," he says. "I wager all of it if you can act like you have some damn sense. No mind games. No sarcasm. No silly little stunts. I'm not even suggesting you last the full three months because there's no way in hell you would. Hell, I'd go as low as a week, but fucking up in one day would be child's play for you. One month. You'd have your full inheritance—"

"And an apology for being so very doubtful of me?" I sound like I'm bluffing.

I'm not. Neither is he.

I can only wait for his response as my chest tightens against a heart that's beating too fast. Bit by bit, my skin feels hotter. It's only by the sheer grace of being near a window that I can blame the breeze for shifting away from him.

"Apology?" Thorny harrumphs. "I'll write it on the fucking wall in my own damn blood if you want. In fact." He laughs again, that maddening sound. I picture him throwing his head back. Maybe he's not so averse to dramatics after all. "I'll even throw in the car."

I bite my lip to disguise my shock. He'd really part with his cherry-red status symbol? In theory. *That's* how convinced he is I'll fail.

Touché, Thorny. A part of me hums—impressed? No, more like...intrigued. Is Elaine's happiness worth so much to him?

"And one more thing?" I turn, schooling every muscle I possess to meet his gaze without flinching. He's stormy again, old Thorny. I'm sliced through like a peeled banana —but he doesn't need to know that. "You give me Thornfield, too. I'd even let you live here...maybe."

His upper lip quirks, but it's in the wrong direction. *Up*, not down. Another fleeting smile catches me off guard.

"Done," he says.

Or at least that's what his words convey. His body language is a mixture of tense shoulders and flexing fingers that curl into and out of fists. Annoyingly, I can't get a read on just what they mean. Nervousness? Anticipation?

"So, what does a good girl do, Daddy?" My finger creeps into my hair before I can stop it. By then, it's too late. He's watching as I twist a curl around my pinkie and another flashback unfurls from the mental crevice I shoved all Thorny memories into.

"She hasn't stopped tugging at her hair since it happened." Grandmama's voice drifted through the doorway, gruff with perpetual disapproval. "The girl might go bald by the time of the funeral. Please…James. Just comfort her, if you can?"

I bit my lip, alarmed by her tone. Grandmama commanded. She never groveled. She never pleaded.

She was never refused.

"No," Thorny said, his voice a disapproving baritone even then. "I can't stay. I'll ask Elaine to look after her."

"Good girls?" the present-day Thorny wonders, still eyeing how my finger is nudging a lock of my hair around and around. He frowns. "A decent human being would go upstairs, change into something appropriate, and eat her goddamn dinner."

He storms into the dining room without taking the time to gloat. Or snicker.

He makes me believe, if only for a second, that he could have meant the dare for real.

I have just seconds to decide whether or not to believe him. I know it. An invisible clock counts down every precious bit of time I waste staring after him. He's lying, of course. I should go in there and overturn every platter of carefully prepared food. Scream. Shout. Cause a scene.

My throat contracts as I approach the staircase instead. Slowly but noisy enough that he can hear and call it off. *You didn't think I was serious, did you, Maryanne? Not stuffy, gruff me?*

I rap my fingers loudly along the banister, listening to the echoing silence. I mount three steps. Three more.

He says nothing. Not even as I enter my room and yank my dress off. *Something appropriate,* he said. Like Elaine's plain, pretty ensemble? I rummage through my ramshackle suitcase until I find a white blouse with a plunging neckline and one of my old plaid skirts from Whorton's.

Decent.

I braid my hair and kick my heels off, leaving my feet bare. Hushed voices seep from the dining room as I return downstairs.

"...starting to wonder if this was a good idea," Elaine says, sounding oh-so worried. "I mean, what if she—"

"It's fine," Thorny says, raising his voice. When I round the corner, I see why: he's facing my direction and most likely heard me coming. His eyebrow arches at my outfit and his lips part, but I beat him to the punch.

"I want to apologize," I say, mustering up my most contrite expression. I even bow my head in shame. It's an Oscar-worthy performance, but no one claps. "I just find that all of this has been so overwhelming…"

"It's all right," Elaine says, regaining her strained grin. "I…I, um, found some things in the fridge and made you a sandwich." She nods toward a delicate creation balanced on a porcelain plate matching the platters. At a glance, it looks to be a lovingly made watercress. She even cut the crusts off.

"Thank you," I say, reclaiming my seat. With two fingers, I nudge the sandwich aside. Then I drag the platter of spaghetti toward me, scoop a heaping pile onto a plate, and shove as many noodles as I can fit onto a fork into my mouth.

Elaine just stares, her smile frozen, her gaze constricted. Thorny, on the other hand, clears his throat—a warning.

So he meant it after all. Be a good girl for a month. He thinks I won't. I bet I can, just for the hell of it.

Forcing myself to swallow, I pat my lips with a napkin. "It tastes marvelous, Ellie."

"You think so?" Elaine turns her wide-eyed gaze to Thorny, who seems more interested in his bottle of wine than validating her culinary skills.

He pours a glass and takes a sip.

"Well, I agree," Jeremy declares, coming to the rescue with that smarmy tone of his. Writers are supposed to be suave, they say. Good with words, but his always sound slimy. "It's damn good spaghetti, Elle. It's not every woman who can cook."

"Thanks." Elaine simpers, fighting a smile. "It's a family recipe on James's side."

"Oh." I nod with mock interest. "Maybe you could teach me? Since I'm family to James as well."

Thorny clears his throat more deeply this time. Less a warning and more an outright threat. *Enough.*

A part of me twists like a piece of bait on a hook. Straining. Flailing. The threat is a leash, yanked at his discretion. Five minutes in and maybe he's right. I couldn't last a week.

"So, Maryanne," Elaine says as if sensing the tension. Like any good housewife, she's adept at changing the subject. "Are you excited to continue with school?"

"School?"

"Yes. You'll be graduating soon, I hear? I know you'll only be here a few months, but I'm sure you'll finish out the year strong."

Finish out the year. My brain seizes on those words and jumps to a dangerous scenario. "Am I going to Walden?" I look from Elaine to Thorny.

"No," Thorny says after draining his wine glass. "You will be tutored by a professor from the school while you're here."

For however long that may be, his disinterested tone tells me.

"But…" I fight to keep my voice at an "appropriate" level. "Why can't I go to the actual school?"

"It's the end of the year, Maryanne," Thorny says. But that's just a lie. The way he meets my gaze directly imparts the truth: *I had to get you an education somewhere, but that doesn't mean near me.*

Indigestion. That's the name I give to the sinking, twisting sensation in my stomach. Mere indigestion and nothing more.

"It's not like I want to go." I roll my eyes. "But I've finished out the year at a new school before."

Many times, in fact. My junior year of high school was spread amongst four different boarding schools and two stints of inpatient psychiatric treatment. I'm a literal expert at slotting myself into a desk and following along with a teacher's droning monotone. You've been to one corporal prison for girls, you've been to them all.

"I can catch up," I say.

"You can't." Thorny doesn't even look up from the depths of his glass. The remaining coating of wine has his full attention, as if he's hoping the last drops will float onto his tongue. "Besides, your grades wouldn't allow you admission anyway."

My teeth clench tight over the half-eaten noodles still in my mouth. I force a swallow down and loosen my jaw. "I have straight A's."

Thorny raises an eyebrow and shifts to face me directly. "Straight A's," he echoes. "And yet you're so far behind that I'll have to pay your tutor double just to give you a prayer of graduating on time. The answer is no."

My fork sprays droplets of sauce onto my lap—I'm gripping it that tightly. "But—"

"The answer is no." His expression all but dares me to challenge him: eyebrows knitted, mouth stretched into a long, flat line.

"Can… May I be excused?"

"No, you may not," he says, reaching for his wine. "Eat your dinner."

"L-look at it this way, Maryanne," Elaine chimes in from her end of the table. "You'll have way more free time. The tutor will only be here for about half the day. You'll have the rest all to yourself."

She makes it sound so damn tempting. A whole handful of hours to play with. All for me. Hours of sulking on her and Thorny's property, knowing they have a calendar hidden somewhere with my birthday circled in the brightest pen ink imaginable.

They'll use me for their own ends, but I'll get some free time out of it. Hooray for me.

"How about I sweeten the pot?" Jeremy makes it sound like he has a golden ticket in his pocket, the key to unlocking all of my hopes and dreams. "I'll send you a signed copy of my latest manuscript. Hot off the presses, before anyone else can even get their hands on it. Elle claims it's another award winner."

"Oh, that's so kind of you, Jeremy." Poor Elaine sounds so impressed. Too impressed. Pink cheeks make her resemble a schoolgirl, singled out for the teacher's attention. "I know I'm not a literary expert"—her gaze flickers toward Thorny, who downs another sip of wine—"but I really did love it."

"It's no problem," Jeremy insists. "Anything for you."

He winks.

I choke.

Ugh.

"Wasn't your last book about a woman who hated her husband so much she got her uterus removed or something?" I ask. *Something, Something Matrimony*, I think it was called. The darling of the NYT bestseller list, and the eventual winner of some stupid literary prize. *Gag. Barf.*

Jeremy's cheeks turn cherry red. "I've heard it described a bit differently than that—"

"We're out of wine," Thorny grunts, rising to his feet. "I'm getting more."

"James…" Elaine watches him go, her cheeks pinker. "Why don't we call it a night? Thank you for coming, Jeremy."

She walks him to the door, but I stay seated, picking at my dinner.

Thorny's little proposition is looking better by the hour. Way more tempting than even making him face me every day at Walden. "I'm sorry" written in blood, he said? *Oh, hell yes.*

So I do what a nice, obedient daughter does best. I shove my pride down my throat with a forkful of spaghetti, and I envision every delicious way I'll ruin James Thorne's perfect life—for funsies.

Not because I actually give a damn. Still, I'll take my time and do it the old-fashioned way.

One bite at a time.

FOUR

hey don't even give me a day to settle in. The moment I wake up, Elaine knocks on my door.

"Your tutor is here, Maryanne," she says. "I'll leave breakfast for you in the study—hope you like eggs. It's the last door on the left downstairs. Good luck!"

I take my sweet time fishing a clean skirt and a shirt from my suitcase. Then I remove the rest of my clothing, revealing what's taken up the bulk of space: a stack of paperbacks with simple covers and pretentious titles. *Wasteland. Murder Town. Swing.*

They're all written by the one and only James Thorne. Each one sports dogeared pages, their covers falling off, the pages yellowed. I grab one at random and flip through it. *Swing.* The last one he's released and the only one he bothered to dedicate.

To the girl with the golden curls: I'm sorry.

Lucky Elaine.

She's already gone when I head downstairs and find a new woman in her place. My tutor is wearing a starched dress suit and a pair of ugly brown loafers two sizes too big. Thorny and Elaine have sequestered her in a spacious office near the back of the house, coincidentally within earshot of both the kitchen and his office.

Just in case she screams.

I forget her name the moment she utters it and spend most of her introduction lecture doodling on the fringes of a notebook with a fancy silver pen that I assume came from Thorny's collection. It's tainted now, forever mine. Over is its life of penning overly analytical novels. It's doomed to draw swirls on line paper in mind-numbing rows.

"Do you have any questions?" the tutor asks after an eternity of boring chatter.

"No," I say, surreptitiously turning the page to a clean one. I flatten my hands over the small round table I'm seated at. It's positioned near a corner, with a tempting view of the beach and the lower balcony from a different angle. Elaine wanders it, murmuring into a cell phone. Every few minutes, she throws her head back to laugh. Thorny's gone. She must be talking to him.

How disgustingly loving.

"Maryanne?" The tutor raps her fingers along the edge of the table. She's frowning, and once again, I feel the tug of Thorny's invisible leash. *Be a good girl.*

"S-sorry." I clamp my teeth to trap any other words behind them. Forcing a smile, I pick my pen up and keep scribbling.

We cover the usual suspects. A bit of math. A bit of science. Finally, English—my one problem subject. The tutor laments that I'm "just a little behind."

"Language is always a tricky subject," she explains, contorting her mouth in a way to convey concern and compassion. Her eyes widen, her lips downturned. She's checking every tick on the list of empathy, but I feel nothing. "Even for children who grew up in bilingual households."

Bilingual. Funny, considering that the only words of French I know are *au revoir*, *non*, and the myriad of ways to convey, *"Go to hell, Charles! And take that little brat with you."*

"I've found that sometimes journaling a little every day can help to strengthen vocabulary and creative writing skills," the tutor says. She rummages through her briefcase and returns with a slim, virgin notebook in the same shade as Thorny's car: cherry red.

"A journal?" It takes effort to school my expression into a simpering grin. Journals are for those whiny bitches in boarding school with no real friends to spill their secrets to. Maybe they got stupid and scribbled down a few things they shouldn't have. One sneaky case of theft later and their silly inner turmoil was the talk of the school.

"Just a few paragraphs a day. We can even discuss them if you want."

I don't need a fucking journal, are the words I bite back. "What should I write about?"

"Anything," the woman says with a shrug. "Anything you'd like. Your hopes. Dreams. What you ate for dinner. I just want you to try to incorporate words or phrases you don't normally use. Let's start with one. How about…" She taps her chin like she's thinking, but it's painfully obvious she already has a phrase in mind. "This is what I discovered about myself today."

My teeth strain against their gums, protesting how hard I'm gritting them. "Okay," I finally say.

"Good. Then we'll continue this tomorrow." The tutor packs up her things and heads for the hallway. In a suspiciously timed coincidence, she nearly runs right into Thorny.

So he is home after all. I sneak a peek from the window, but Elaine's still on the balcony. One of her hands plays with the ends of her hair as she leans against the railing, speaking into her cell phone.

Odd.

"How was she?" Thorny asks the tutor. Suspicion laces his tone.

I guess I'm not the only one struggling with my good behavior. His nonverbal cues cut right to the point: *Give me a reason to break this off. Just a single one.*

"She did great," my tutor says. "Same time tomorrow, Maryanne?"

"Yes," I say cheerfully. "Thank you, ma'am."

Thorny glances me over, his eyes narrowed. "I'll walk you out, Jane." He offers his arm to the tutor and they head toward the front of the house. Where he'll question her again, more earnestly. *Be honest. You can tell me. What asinine thing did she do today?*

Asinine. It's one of the new words sprinkled on a vocabulary list I find tucked inside the cover of my journal. Asinine. Beatific. Egregious. Cautious. Denigrate…

Printed at the bottom of the sheet is my phrase for the day. What have I discovered about myself?

Well, for one, being good is fucking hard. The clock on the wall claims it's barely noon. It feels later than that. An eternity since Thorny made his bet.

One month.

I have to sequester myself in the tutoring room just to last another hour. It's not my fault. There are so many naughty things around here that a bad girl could stick her nose into. Nosy little questions, for instance.

Elaine puts her phone down, her faint smile fading. Thorny comes up behind her and her grip tightens on the banister as she looks back. She must say something to him, because he shakes his head and moves to stand at the opposite end of the railing. When Elaine faces the water again, her tiny smile is gone.

I don't realize I'm tapping my pen against the journal's cover until I miss and strike the table. *Thwack!* The noise reminds me of thunder. It'll probably rain again today, erasing the hard work the sun put into drying out the fields and the lonely beach.

I've been into metaphors a lot lately, so I can't help feeling as though the current weather is a giant one for what my presence does to Thorny and Elaine. It looms overhead, stealing the sunlight from their bright, cheerful lives. *Boo hoo.*

Thorny bet that I couldn't last the week.

But can he?

He shifts as if sensing my naughty thoughts and his head swivels in my direction. I swear he's glaring at me through the window, daring me to test his limits.

But I don't.

I merely tap the nib of my pen against a blank page, mulling over my assignment. Good, dutiful daughters do their homework. They journal down their feelings in nice, neat paragraphs with no concern that they might be read by anyone else down the line. Naïveté is the word *du jour*.

That's the trap of a diary: they're practically designed to be read. This bright-red cover screams intrigue to anyone willing to turn the page—and everyone knows that secrets make the best weapon fodder. I learned that the hard way. Those written about are forever trapped on the page, locked within a certain context or moment with no shading to color the perspective. Just emotion.

It's the most dangerous thing of all. Friends can seem more nefarious on paper. Cool teachers might be given more scrutiny.

And stuffy, overbearing uncles might not seem so perfect after all.

*E*laine promised I'd have "the rest of the day" to myself like some alluring present, just for me. In practice, there's nowhere to go. No gossip to overhear. No headmistresses with buttons to push.

Fuck all. There's just a boring house to explore and offices to sneak into. Thorny doesn't even bother to lock his, but that's just a part of his game: even the drawers are empty in here. The books on the shelves aren't his. The computer only holds generic programs, and I can't even find the hint of a manuscript when I peek through the files.

He's called my bluff, old Thorny, and he's hidden his toys without even giving me the chance to play with them.

Annoyed, I find myself wandering the property again. I return to the tree house. Get bored. Wander down a path leading to the beach.

Find sand.

Return to the main house.

Find it empty.

Wash, rinse, and repeat.

By dinnertime, I'm convinced I'll die of boredom in a month. So what does it matter if I break the rules now? They both make it so fucking tempting.

Elaine floats into the dining room carrying a platter of baked chicken and a bowl of salad balanced on both hands. Gracefully, she sets them in the center of the table. Her yellow dress makes her shine as purplish clouds outside obscure the real sun. She's a pretty, lifeless substitute, taking her place at one end of the table.

Thorny, her surly storm cloud, takes the opposite end.

Like a good daughter, I stay in the middle, fidgeting like lightning caught between them.

"How was your day?" Elaine wonders as she serves herself. "Jane's a wonderful teacher. She helped me with a few articles once upon a time."

That's right. Elaine writes too. She "writes" for fancy feminist journals that make more room for her pictures than her actual articles. She's social justice eye candy.

"It was fine." I nibble on a piece of chicken. Choke it down. Thorny's watching, I realize, waiting for a flaw to pounce on. Meeting his gaze, I grin as sweetly as I can. So good am I. "Marvelous, actually. I learned so much—"

"Maryanne," Thorny interjects. It's not so much of a warning as a gentle tug on that stupid invisible leash. *Watch yourself.*

Ignoring him, I face Elaine. "How was your day, Ellie?"

"Not too bad," she replies, beaming. "I'm just getting my final notes together. I go on assignment in a few months."

Assignment. "You're leaving?"

"Just for work, and long after you graduate." She sounds so excited. So proud. "I'm examining the lives of some of the indigenous cultures of Central America."

Oh. All of a sudden, the scene on the balcony makes more sense.

"Were you talking to a subject on the phone earlier?" I ask.

Because good, real people notice the actions of those around them and parrot them back. To make them feel seen. Heard. It's called reflecting, according to my therapist. It lets the people around you know that you care. It's nice.

"A what?" Elaine goes three shades paler than her thick screen of makeup. She's a golden face perched atop an ivory body. "I... Um, yes," she says, her gaze flicking toward Thorny and back. "Just a subject. A friend."

"You're going on assignment again?" Thorny makes the question sound oh-so harmless.

But where I accidentally stepped into a verbal bear trap, he throws a grenade.

"We t-talked about this." Elaine flattens her hands against the table, fighting to keep her smile wide. "Belize. For six weeks. We *talked* about this."

"Have we?" Thorny cocks an eyebrow and pushes back from the table. "I'll be in the study."

He leaves, and Elaine clears her throat, piling salad onto her plate. "We'll just…finish eating," she says. "Tell me more about your day, huh?"

"It was fine," I say.

And nothing else.

We play our charade in silence as Thorny's footsteps echo throughout the house, making it very clear that he's not in the study. He's heading toward the balcony. Even as the rain falls.

He stands out there and lets every drop pelt him on the way down.

SIX

*D*reams are the catalyst for naughty behavior. It's why I'm prescribed one hundred and fifty milligrams of trazodone before I go to bed. Which I wash down with five milligrams of Ambien, ten milligrams of melatonin, and fifty milligrams of Benadryl.

I take them every night, as diligently as a five-year-old chews their vitamin gummies. A handful a day keeps the doctor away.

But, tonight, something seeps through. I'm back there, if only for a second. In that house. That room.

Daddy's cologne tickles my nose, decidedly off. There's some sharper smell overpowering the crisp Calvin Klein. The same way Mama smelled after one of her dinner parties, when her words slurred into a sloppy mixture of French and English.

Boozy.

He should be awake by now. I'm going to be late for ballet. Irritated, I march around the leather chaise Mama likes to lounge on, toward the massive closet at the back of their suite.

I hear it first. That slow, unnatural swish. The creak of the clothing rack straining...

A shadow flickers just beyond the open closet door. The light is on.

"Daddy?"

He doesn't say anything.

And then I look up…

"What the hell do you mean '*I should have known*'?"

I blink my eyes open and find a twisted layer of cotton cocooning my limbs. It's dark in the room, and something soft tickles my face when I try to sit up. Canopy, I remember as my heart races. I'm in Thorny's house, in my perfect new room. Rain lashes at the windows—but that's not the storm that woke me up.

It's the one playing out down below in the form of shouting voices and shattering glass.

"Keep your voice down," Elaine pleads. "And I've mentioned it. Maybe you forgot, but I *did*—"

"He'll be there, won't he?" Thorny phrases the question like a whip. "I was wondering why you had the nerve to invite him to dinner."

"Don't do this." Elaine gasps. "James, please—"

"Will he?"

"He's sponsoring the trip, but it's not—"

"So why wait a few months?" Thorny demands. "For my sake? Because of *her*?"

"It's just business!"

"Sure it is." He laughs, and goosebumps prickle my skin, chafing against the sheets. "So why wait? Be my fucking guest. Go now."

"James!"

"Go be with him. Don't let me stop you," Thorny taunts. "Go perform your 'business.'"

"Just keep your voice down," Elaine stage-whispers, but she's louder than he is. "What if Maryanne hears you?"

"Don't. Don't you dare use her as your excuse."

"*You're* the one who brought her here," Elaine snipes. "Why? Because you wanted to add gasoline to the fire? I'm not the one using her as an excuse… James, please! Where are you going?"

"Out."

Two sets of footsteps race toward, I assume, the foyer. A heavier set leads the way as lighter, quicker steps desperately gain on them.

"We need to talk about this, please. Just listen to me—"

"Call him," Thorny says over the sound of a door opening. "Tell him you can be there by the end of the week. You have my *blessing*."

The door slams shut.

Elaine sighs. Then sobs, but in smothered little snippets. Eventually, she wanders deeper into the house, though never upstairs.

She's watching from a window, I bet. Waiting for him to come back.

I burrow beneath the blankets, smothering a laugh into the sheets. *Oh, Elaine. I learned that lesson years ago.*

He never does.

The thing about bad dreams is that they linger, infesting everything. All the dark thoughts you fight so hard to shove into that deep, dank hole in the pit of your mind escape.

Only when you wake up, the rest of the world pretends like none of the bad things ever happened. You just have to choke on the memories all day until they finally crawl back to where they came from.

"Good morning!" Elaine greets as I descend the stairs. She's smiling, her hair perfectly coiffed, her dress a flowy, flouncy pink.

She was wrong the other day. I look nothing like the parent who should not be named.

She does, superficial happiness and all.

"Jane should be here any moment," she says. "You can wait for her in the study. I have some errands to run, but I'll be back tonight, and we'll have a chat. Just you and me. What do you think?"

Her white teeth sparkle in the sun, her makeup flawless.

"Okay," I say.

"Great!" She skips through the front door, and I watch from the window as her shoulders slump the moment she descends the front steps. Thorny's car isn't the one waiting out front for her; it's a black one driven by someone I can't see. Just like that, she's gone in a flash.

Thorny isn't home, either. I can smell it. The air tastes different without his signature scent of wine and cologne. Mommy and Daddy left the baby home alone.

I can't resist. I creep up to their room, scouring the neatly made bed and the immaculate closet for clues. Maybe they had make-up sex? That's what grown-ups do, after all. Scream at each other and fuck.

My parents did it.

"Don't pretend like you care, *mon cher*," my mother used to snipe at my father. "You'll rant and rave, and then we'll fuck. *Ça va*? You never change."

But Thorny's not the make-up-sex type. He's way too brooding for that. No. He prefers to lord his power over those who dare to cross him. For days. For years, even. Silence is his favorite weapon, withheld at will. A truly cruel punishment of his creation would be this: disappearing.

The door to the balcony creaks. When I tiptoe toward it, I find it unlocked. Stepping onto the deck, I spot a hazy figure wandering the beach, sandwiched between ocean and sand.

"He hates going down to the beach," Elaine had said.

I guess Thorny has his own secrets.

I don't know how long I watch him. When I finally hear the sound of knocking on the front door, my face feels hot, inflamed by the sun. Jane the tutor is waiting on the front steps, her briefcase in hand.

Together, we work through mind-numbing assignments until Jane asks to see my notebook. When she realizes that it's still empty, she frowns, disappointed.

"I want you to try writing something down now," she instructs, placing the book in front of me. "You don't even have to show me what it says. Just practice."

Practice. I bite my lower lip and scribble down the first sentence that comes to mind: *This is fucking stupid. Stupid. STUPID. StUpId.*

"Now, write about something else," she prompts. "Something maybe you can't say out loud. We can keep these journals private, if you'd like. Just try forming words in a new way."

A new way.

My father didn't slip and fall, I write. *He hanged himself.*

That's the naughty truth I'm not allowed to say out loud. There. I lift my pen and wait for the freedom that Jane seems to think can be experienced by scratching out words in watery ink. Nothing yet.

I am bored, I write. Still nothing.

"I think this is a good place for our final lesson," Jane suggests. "I want you to use our last hour to write. Anything at all. Just get the words out. Play with them. Maybe try writing a story if you'd like—"

"Like my uncle?"

"Well, yes," she says, smiling. She thinks it's a fitting aspiration. "Though it's been so long since he's written anything. Maybe you can trigger his inspiration? You probably have his flair for drama."

"I'll write something different, then." I sound so unimpressed.

Thorny has been on the *New York Times* bestselling blah blah blah list more than once. His work inspires legions of fans who love reading lame, by-the-book crime dramas without an ounce of tawdry romance or sex. It's because Thorny is such a creative mind that Grandmama thought he'd communicate best with a traumatized child. He could tell me fantastical stories to take my mind off the horror I witnessed. Tales of unicorns and princesses who vomit glitter. Normal stuff.

I never told her what tales Thorny wove for me instead. Like when he sat me down, looked me dead in my innocent, teeny eyes, and declared, "I am not your father. Wanting me to be isn't healthy, Maryanne. Just stop it!"

Lifting my pen, I try to take Jane's advice.

I hate James Thorne. This time, I do feel something: a prickle in my chest. Probably indigestion—I bet those eggs Elaine made for breakfast were poisoned. Sighing, I rip the page out and crumble it into a ball. I aim for the wastebasket in the corner and miss. *Swish.* The ball bounces away, and I turn my attention to a brand-new page.

Unbeknownst—another new vocabulary word—to Jane, I spend the rest of her hour drawing stick people in the fringes of the margins. They meander through their happy stick lives, keeping the other figures at a safe distance with their linear appendages. Finished, I take a walk around the house and consider throwing my journal into the ocean.

I start toward the beach but return to the house when I realize how damn hot it is. So hot that my sandals stick to the bottoms of my feet. Seeking the AC, I wander into the living room. Where I find Thorny scowling on the balcony, a beer in hand.

He sips.

I sneak onto a chair near the window and scribble a doodle onto a page, watching him all the while.

Sip. Sip.

Scribble. Scribble.

I don't know what gives me away. Maybe I'm writing too loudly. Breathing too loudly. Existing too loudly. He turns and glowers when he finds me, my face pressed against the glass. Tossing his head back, he drains the beer and knocks the bottle over the railing. Deliberately.

Uh-oh. My stomach clenches as he marches toward me. I stand, backing out of his reach the moment he yanks on the sliding glass door. *Slam!* If I had been any closer, my fingers would have been caught.

"Hello, Uncle James!" Mustering up a cheerful smile, I fold my hands primly over my lap. "Where's Elaine?"

He says nothing. But he doesn't move, either. No. Some other emotion has him rooted here, breathing in the same air I am. His eyes gleam, electrified.

Uh-oh. Thorny's angry.

"So much for the fucking bet. How long have you known?" he wonders through clenched teeth. "Was that one of the first things you sussed out, huh? Did you go through her phone?" He snatches my wrist and I wince. Too tight.

"Ow!"

The second I resist, his fingers latch onto my wrist bone like a vise. "Was it her messages? How?"

"You're hurting me!" I try to pull away.

He tugs right back, dragging me a step toward him. Up this close, I realize that he's not cold, callous Thorny now. He's serious, spiteful Uncle James.

"I bet you couldn't wait to rub my nose in it, could you?"

Elaine. He's talking about Elaine. Their hushed conversation wasn't a dream after all. Naughty girls shouldn't eavesdrop though, so I school my face into a mask.

"I don't know what you're talking about—"

"Don't play dumb with me!" He's shouting. "You want to know the truth? Everyone told me to just keep you locked in the fucking psych ward. Refuse to take you back. Let the state have you. *Everyone.*"

"So, why didn't you listen, then?" Heat sinks into my skin, creeping through every nerve and pore. I yank my arm and he lets go only to snatch my forearm in an even tighter grasp. I stagger, forced to brace my hand over an end table for balance. "Stop!"

"You've been nothing but a burden on this entire fucking family since day one—"

"Get off me!" I dig my feet into the carpet and wrench on my wrist, leaning away from him. "Let me go!"

"I should," he agrees. "Everyone else is done with you. Lily won't even welcome you into her home. Caroline's kids haven't seen their father in three months. But I took you in anyway—"

"Why?" I stop resisting. Turn to face him. Smile. "Because you're such a *good* uncle?"

"You have no fucking idea, do you?" He looks shocked, old Thorny. I'm so stupid that he just can't deal. "You want to ruin my marriage like you did Caroline's? Do your worst. That's the only way someone like you can feel joy, isn't it?"

"Someone like me?" My throat feels too tight and the words come out wrong. Too soft. Hoarse.

"You heard me. Oh, that's right. We aren't supposed to say it out loud. What you really are." He looks me over and scoffs. "A selfish, spoiled little psychopath."

He lets me go and stalks toward the archway, probably to hunt for more wine. Halfway there, he pauses to snatch something from his pocket. He throws it at me. A wad of paper bounces off my chest, landing in front of my toes.

It's my crumbled-up assignment. *I hate James Thorne.*

"You just can't get over it, can you?" He shakes his head, overwhelmed with my stupidity. "People die every damn day, and you don't see everyone else holding on to grudges. Festering over childish little fantasies—"

"But I'm a psychopath," I parrot tonelessly. "Remember? And do you know what psychopaths do?" I swear we turn at the same time, honing in on a porcelain vase sitting prettily on the mantel. I lunge for it, sensing him right on my heels.

"Don't you dare!"

He's too late. I snatch the vase by the neck and pitch it toward the beautiful view of the ocean. *Smash!* It shatters into pieces.

So much for being a good girl.

"That's enough!" He grabs my shoulder again, dragging me toward the couch at the opposite end of the room.

I scream. Scratch. Dig my heels in. He's relentless, yanking me across the carpet when I lose my balance.

"You want me to be your fucking father?" he asks, shoving me onto the couch cushions. "Fine. I'll do what he should have fucking done a long time ago!"

I kick at his arm as his fingers come for me, latching onto the hem of my skirt.

And then I freeze. My mind goes blank. *Poof.*

Uncontested, Thorny wrenches my skirt up to my lower back, allowing the cool air to tickle me through my cotton undies. They're too thin. The baby-pink frilly kind no one was ever supposed to see.

When a hard palm lands against my ass, I feel it all. My teeth clatter as my hands grip a pillow in shock.

"Is this what you fucking wanted?" he shouts, striking again. *Thwack.*

Thwack.

Thwack.

Each sting jolts through my veins, merciless. One. Five. Ten. The exertion has him cursing every time his hand meets my ass.

"Damn it! Maybe if Charles beat your ass, you wouldn't be such a little—"

He stops suddenly. Steps back, letting me slump forward. I watch him stare down at his hand, his mouth open, his eyes like slits as he looks at me. *Really* looks at me.

Then I hear it. Soft, little footsteps creeping up the walkway outside, crunching over the path. Elaine. Mommy has returned. Mustn't let her see the mess.

Thorny is panting, his chest heaving, his face reddened and splotchy. "Get—"

I don't listen. I'm on my feet, shoving away from him. To the stairs. Up. Into my room, slamming the door in my wake. Twisting the lock.

Screaming.

Screaming.

Just as a door opens downstairs, I break off, biting so hard at the back of my hand to keep quiet that I taste salt. Elaine calls out words I can't decipher, and someone gruffly barks a response. Two sets of footsteps drift toward opposite parts of the house.

And then there's just silence. So loud that I can't hear anything but the *lack* of noise. No honking horns to block out my ragged breathing. No distant shouting to obscure the scratching hiss my hair makes as I twist it around. Around. Around.

No Thorny spitting in my face all those means words everyone else thinks but never says.

You're a selfish, spoiled little psychopath.

The joke's on him; antisocial personality disorder is rarely diagnosed in someone below the age of eighteen. It's a stigma, you see. Can't call them sociopaths. What about *borderline?* Sure. They can slap that term on your medical file and use it as an excuse to psycho-splain away all of your problems, fears, and anger.

You're the broken one. It doesn't matter why you scream. Or shout. Or throw things when people refuse to fucking listen.

I'm the only one with a diagnosis.

And the truly manipulative, selfish, psychopathic thing to do would be to yank my skirt off and shove it onto the floor. With one hand, I tug my panties down while grabbing my cell phone in the other. I have to stand awkwardly and hold it at an angle to get the right shot.

Redness paints my right buttock. And it still hurts. I try to sit on the mattress and wince.

All I have to do is send this picture to Mr. Lawyer or the police. *He hit me,* I'd wail. *Like an animal. It was so, so, so scary...*

My fingers dance over the right buttons, but I don't press them. Yet. My brain skips ahead, imagining how this scenario will unfold. Thorny will get investigated. Maybe even charged. He'll lose his job. His reputation will take a ding.

But voices would whisper: *Oh, that little bitch? She deserved it.*

I drop the phone, lying back across the bed. A spanking scandal might affect him for a year or two, but then everyone would forget the whiny little psychopath who called "wolf." No…

James Thorne deserves a much worse punishment.

I brought that stupid red journal upstairs, I realize. I pick it up and drop it so that it falls open to a clean page. Then I hunt for a pen. Pressing the nib into the paper, I hesitate.

Tell a story, Jane suggested.

The best ones start with *once upon a time*—like mine. Once upon a time, something terrible happened to a young girl named Maryanne. Only one person in the world could comfort her.

And he did.

Until he realized she was tainted. Dirty. Broken.

So he threw her away.

Adjusting my grip on the pen, I start writing.

Dear diary,

He lifted my skirt. Told me not to tell.

Should I?

SEVEN

I don't go down for dinner. Instead, I take my sleeping aid cocktail, and I don't dream, either. When I wake up, sunlight sears through the drapes with a vengeance.

I get dressed in a shirt and a pair of jeans. As I drag the waistband over my hips, I wince. Rather than fixate on why, I grab my diary and head downstairs.

It's a brand-new day.

"Maryanne?" Elaine sticks her head into the hall from the living room as I descend the bottom step. She's wearing gray. A dress that doesn't swish when she walks but remains stiff, with a hem reaching just above her knees. Her hair is slicked back, her makeup minimal. Pale skin enhances the redness in her eyes.

But even still. She wears her trademark smile.

"Can we talk?" she asks.

My first thought is that she knows. Old Thorny came clean about his naughty behavior. Then they reconciled, even about the mysterious friend luring her away on business trips. Together, they reached the obvious conclusion as to the catalyst for all their problems: me.

They fought, but eventually, Elaine decided it would be best if I left.

Though, in that case, Thorny would be the one to gloat…

Curious, I follow Elaine into the living room and spot the suitcase leaning against the couch. Hers not mine.

"I…I've decided to go away on my business trip a little early. I'll be back before your birthday though." She lifts her lips, baring her pearly white teeth. Then she sighs, letting the expression fall. "Can I have a hug before I go?"

A hug. Two arms extended. Closeness maintained for exactly five seconds. Supposedly, they make people feel something. Safe? Loved?

Or, in Elaine's case, less guilt. I don't think it works. She draws back, turning away from me.

"I'll leave my number," she says. "Call me if anything—"

"You mean…I'm staying?"

Of course not. I wait for her to say as much, doing Thorny's dirty work for him. *The lawyer will be here in an hour. I'm sorry, Maryanne.*

"Y-yes." Elaine blinks. "It's just for a few weeks. James… He'll look after you." She stoops for the handle of her suitcase and starts for the door. Before opening it, she looks back, hunting for a figure who doesn't appear to send her off. "Goodbye…"

I watch her leave, but it isn't until the door slams shut that it sinks in.

Mommy left the nest, leaving me alone with Daddy.

Leaving me *alone*.

A surreal feeling washes over me. This hazy, sleepy sensation like I'm not really awake. This isn't really happening. I felt it only a handful of times before.

The first time I woke up in a hospital to some stern-faced psychiatrist informing me I'd tried to kill myself.

Before that. At the funeral all those years ago, maybe in this very spot, when everything inside me came to a boiling point and all I could do was scream.

Oh. And that one time I wandered into a closet and found my father hanging from a necktie.

Those times felt a lot like this.

"It's called dissociating," one of my many therapists explained. "Whenever you feel that way, try to resist it. Ground yourself, Maryanne."

Apparently, dissociating can make one impulsive.

It doesn't really hit home until I enter the entryway, hearing my footsteps echo. From a distance, I catch the sound of a car driving away. Just for a few weeks, she said. But her eyes told differently.

All isn't what it seemed in paradise.

Someone broke the rules.

Was it him?

I march into their bedroom as if the furniture might talk and give me an answer. The bed is still made. A stale scent taints the air. They haven't slept in here in days.

The door to the balcony is open. Thorny glowers at the skyline, drinking wine straight from the bottle. The harder the wind blows off the ocean, the more he drinks. Sip. Sip. Sip. The liquid dribbles shamelessly down his chin. It's barely nine in the morning but, as the sun struggles to climb to its midmorning perch, he continues to drink.

And read. There's something clutched in his other hand. A tiny, red book opened to the first page.

"You think this—" He cocks his head in my direction, his eyes bloodshot, his smile crooked. He lifts my journal and gives it a shake, making the pages strain against the breeze. "You *think* this will work?" he wonders. "Framing me as some kind of pervert? Nice try."

He sets the wine bottle down and rips my page clean from the book. After balling it in a fist, he feeds it to the wind, letting it carry the white ball over into a field.

"But not good enough. If you're going to use my name, you might as well put some fucking flair into it. Here." He whips the book at me and I barely manage to catch it. Stinging fingers clutch it to my chest. "Get a pen. No, wait." He snatches a black one from his pocket and throws it to me as well. "*He lifted my skirt,*" he parrots, "*Told me not to tell.* No one would believe that. Describe it. Now." He jerks his chin to a lounger positioned to face the view. "Sit."

Nerves go haywire beneath my skin. He's a different Thorny altogether today. Someone I don't recognize, with a mangy five-o'clock shadow and unkempt hair. He reeks of wine and is wearing the same clothes from the other day, but his suit jacket is unbuttoned to reveal the shirt underneath. It's wrinkled.

"I told you to sit."

He advances a step and my knees contort, pitching me onto the lounger.

"Write," he snaps. "But not in pathetic little sentences. *Describe* it. How I touched you. What you felt." He laughs as my cheeks catch fire, unbearably hot. "You can't, can you? You want to play the little girl who cried molestation, but you can't even describe what it fucking *feels* like." He shakes his head and snatches up the wine bottle, taking a sip right from the rim. "And this is the same girl who what? Got kicked out of boarding school for fucking some kid in the principal's office?"

He throws the bottle so hard that it ricochets off the siding of the house but doesn't break. It rolls across the balcony instead and slips between gaps in the railing. A second later, there's a smash.

"Jane couldn't make it today," Thorny tells me as he lumbers into the bedroom. "So consider that your fucking assignment. Make up a lie worthy of being told."

He slams the door after him. In fact, I think he locks it, trapping me on the balcony. The same way my mother used to lock me out of her room when she grew bored of me.

It's what adults do.

Barricade themselves against annoying things.

Ignore them.

Then leave them behind.

He touched me, even though I told him to stop. He could feel me shiver. I know he could. His fingers sank into the pleats of my skirt anyway, winding up the fabric despite how I flinched.

Uncles aren't supposed to be like this. They shouldn't breathe heavily against your ear as they ram their hands against your thigh. They shouldn't linger there, letting their heat sink through your—

No. I break off, slashing through the entire sentence. Gritting my teeth, I try again. Tell a lie worth telling. How did I feel, preyed upon by my big, scary uncle Thorny?

Well, like a psychopath.

You're a liar, he told me. *No one will believe it, even if I—*

Ugh! I tear the page out and rip it into thirds. Fourths. Slivers. Confetti. I watch as the white dots sprinkle the wood at my feet, dancing in the wind. Within seconds, they're in every which direction and there's no way to ever put them back together again.

Screw Thorny. He thinks he has the upper hand. Maybe he does. But hands are made for slapping—and I know firsthand what it feels like to do so. When the flat of your palm strikes flesh, the blow hurts you just as much as it does them. You merely pretend not to show it.

It's all a part of the game.

He wants me to be convincing. But to whom? One naughty word in his headmaster's ear and Thorny's job is forfeit. I tell myself that over and over as I watch the door, daring myself to see if he really did leave it unlocked. So what if he didn't?

I could climb down from here, even if he did sink so low. In fact, I will. I'm not afraid. Upon standing, I approach the railing and survey the lower level. It's the same layout as this one, just larger. There are loungers perfect for landing on if I lower myself far enough.

Setting my sights on the nearest one, I throw my journal onto it. Then I climb over the railing, dangling my legs above the lounge chair.

Piece of cake.

Inhaling raggedly, I close my eyes and prepare to jump. I should count to ten or something. One. Two…

My fingers slip. Gravity grabs me by the ankles, yanking hard. *Bang!* I hear the thud before I feel the pain. Blinding. Splitting.

Black.

The sun is spitting in my eyes when I finally peel them open. Taunting me. I start to roll onto my side but wind up staring at my arm. My hands.

They're painted red. Merry Christmas. It's mistletoe red. On my skirt. The wood of the deck. Dripping down my nose, onto my tongue. It has a taste: yummy salty flavor. *Uh-oh.* My fingers fly to my forehead as if knowing something I don't.

Ow. Pain, pain, pain no matter where I touch.

"Maryanne!"

Thudding footsteps make me look up. Thorny's racing toward me, stopping short when he sees my face.

His eyes go bug-wide, his mouth dropping open. "What the hell…" Something makes him pause, an eyebrow raised. Then the alarm disappears, and he scoffs. "I see you improved the makeup this time."

Makeup? Bright, cherry-red makeup, pooling in puddles as I try to stand. The sun starts stabbing me, making me wince as the house becomes a tilt-a-whirl, rocking left to right.

"I preferred the bruises," Thorny adds, staring down at me from his Romanesque nose. "They looked way more realistic."

More realistic than what? My stomach churns, telling me I don't want to know.

"Elaine's not here to fall for your game, you do realize."

Oh. I stop moving. He thinks I'm faking, staging another dramatic scene.

"At least you came running," I point out. But my voice sounds funny. My tongue feels heavy, and fear conjures up a million potential reasons why.

I need to see a mirror. My limbs rush to propel me upright, but everything moves out of sync. I have to brace my hand flat against the floor. Flatter. Try to stand. Too fast. Sit down. Try again.

"Very convincing," Thorny exclaims, clapping. "When you're done, I'll be in the study."

He marches off, huffing and puffing. Good. That means I can crawl into the living room alone. Only the room elongates with every inch I gain, stretching. Transforming. It's an endless hall that takes an eternity to pass.

The stairs are ten times taller than they should be. I try to climb the first one, but my hands miss. I'm on my knees again.

"Maryanne?" He sounds different now.

Something nudges my shoulder. At least I think...

I'm too tired. "I need to go upstairs," I say—to my legs, not to him. Move. *Get up.* "I need to move."

"Maryanne?" Warm fingers sink through my hair and come away dripping scarlet. "Shit."

He looks worried now, Old Thorny. It transforms him once again into someone else—but I've met this man before. A long, long time ago when my entire world was upended.

He bundled me in his arms like he does now, holding me tight.

"It'll be okay," he told me then. "I'm here. Do you hear me? I'm here."

And I believed him once…

Never twice.

EIGHT

We're in the car. He's driving too fast and talking too loudly. "Say something," he commands. "Stay awake. Talk to me."

Talk? It's one thing I never learned how to do. Not in all of my therapy sessions or those brief meetings with my psychologist. I learned to color, paint, and channel my emotions into productive pursuits.

But converse?

Normal people could do that. *I* needed medication.

"Look at me." Thorny takes one hand from the steering wheel and snaps his fingers—but the car starts to drift, forcing him to grab the wheel again. "Fuck." He risks driving one-handed to flick the dials of the radio. Angry rock blares, but he doesn't change the channel. "Stay awake!"

But maybe I don't want to. This could all be a dream. I want it to be. A dreary, dizzying dream.

Because, otherwise, it hurts too much. Pain makes people make stupid mistakes. Like listen, sinking into the cadence of a voice hoarse with concern. A stupid person might believe it's real this time…

"Maryanne! Open your eyes," he snaps. "Do you hear me? You never can listen, can you? Fuck, why did you even want to come back? They gave you a choice. I know they did."

They. My treatment team. And a choice they did give: stay there in fancy rehab until my birthday and interact with other damaged dolls my own age or be shipped away to a relative who never wanted me.

"You hate being here," Thorny points out. "So why stay?"

My brain might be melting, dripping down my nose, but I know just what answers he's come up with on his own. I wanted him to take me in, but why?

To ruin his marriage, of course.

To destroy his career.

To make him regret the day I was ever thrust into his life.

Or maybe it's a lot simpler. And pathetic.

My laugh trickles out of me as my eyes drift shut. "I don't hate you. All…all I wanted was *you*."

"Look at me, Maryanne."

My eyes snap open, but the world looks different. Too bright. Blinding. My eyelids flutter as Thorny stares down on me, haloed by white light. *Am I dead?*

No. Unless hell is a cacophony of voices.

"Can I get a heart rate?" someone demands.

"Send for an MRI and CT—but first, we need to stabilize her neck."

Stabilize. The job of a hideous, orange object lowered over my torso. I shake my head, but someone grabs my shoulders, pinning me down to wrap that object around my throat.

"No!" I squirm, kicking, bucking. "Get off me!"

My neck. It's around my neck. Tightening. Choking. Suffocating.

Tight like a blue necktie with orange swirls. The one me and Mama picked out for Father's Day. He tied it to two more, but that was the one suspending him. Cutting off his windpipe.

The one that killed him.

"Get off me!" I don't care who I grab with my nails or hit with my feet. I can't let them choke me. I can't.

"Maryanne!"

God, it's *his* voice. Not again. So calm when all I want to do is scream. So gentle and deep—it's all I can hear.

"Listen to me," he commands. "I've got you. It's all right. I'm here."

The limb I'm attacking now grips me tight. A hand—his, holding me.

I know it's a lie. I *know*.

But my traitorous ears ensure I take in every word.

"I'm here," he says. "I'm here. I won't let anything happen to you. You're safe…"

NINE

Subdural hematoma is my new phrase for the day. That, along with other juicy terms. Like the *lacerations* beneath my left eye and my bottom lip. *Mild concussion*. Twenty stitches to hold my head together in total.

Oh, and *observation*. Twenty-four hours with my neck in a brace.

They drug me with something. Happy, calming medicine that makes it easier to sleep once the doctor is convinced I won't die. There are no nightmares here. Just noise— beeping and chattering, constant noise.

As the drugs wear off, my thoughts reform from snippets and random realizations. I'm in a room now, I think, admitted overnight.

Oh, the memories. Lying here conjures a few—like the first time I woke up in a hospital like this, thrown into the locked psych ward.

You take too many of your mommy's secret stash of Ambien and it's a suicide attempt, or so they say. Then, two years later, you get a little too handsy with a knife and you're automatically deemed "a danger to yourself and others."

They all came that first time. Grandmama. Elaine. Even Lily, Caroline, and Marcia.

Everyone but Thorny. He was in New York, they told me. On a business trip. He'd be back.

But, even then, I knew the truth: he saw through my act. Good, old Thorny wouldn't let himself be suckered in by my cry for help.

Not even when those cries turned into screams.

I could never fool him, no siree. Because everything I did was *always* in the context of craving attention. From him, only him.

I bet he called Elaine first thing. She must be the one softly snoring somewhere nearby. Poor little housewife. She had to tear herself away from her affair, all because of a silly Maryanne stunt.

But at least he's gone again. I'm still high enough to comfort myself with the same old lie: it doesn't matter. Maybe I'll forget the words he said. How he said them. Maybe this time they won't fucking mean anything. They won't haunt me to the point that an army of sleeping medication is needed to block them out.

I'm here.

I won't let anything happen to you.

You're safe.

Lies.

Lies.

Lies.

My eyes sting as I peel them open and sneaky moisture trickles down my cheeks. At least the appearance of tears might make Elaine pity me enough to leave me alone, like a good pet rock.

I tilt my head just enough to look for her. Someone's slumped in an armchair positioned near my bed. They're snoring, but the gruff hum sounds way too masculine to belong to Elaine. Then I feel it: a hand in mine. Large and rough with age, callused by use. I'm holding it way too tight.

I pry my fingers loose one by one, but my visitor stirs the second I let him go.

"Are you awake?"

Am I? I try to pinch myself just to be sure, but my arms don't budge. My body is an unresponsive blob resistant to any command I issue it. So I sigh.

He does too. "They wanted to keep you overnight," he explains. Thorny. There are shadows hammered beneath his eyes, illuminated by faint, gray light sneaking in through the windows.

It's late. Or early. I can't tell. He's still wearing the same clothes he was before, only now they're decorated in crusty, red patches of dried blood.

It must be early then, the next day.

"Where's Elaine?" I don't like how fragile my voice sounds. The neck brace is a cage, making it hard to suck in enough air. I squirm, desperate to escape the pressure.

"They did all the scans and don't think there's any damage," Thorny says without answering my question. "We can take the brace off—"

"Yes." I finally remember how to make my body move. My hands claw at the sides of the brace, but steadier fingers than mine are needed to finally unlock it—and he actually helps me.

Freedom. I gulp a breath and release it slowly. Then I remember who's watching and stop myself from clutching my throat with both hands. "I see my makeup skills fooled you all," I quip.

His nostrils twitch. To fulfill his role, he should say something stern and scolding. How dare I joke at a time like this?

But he doesn't. Silence is more irritating than his disdain in the end. My skin prickles, itching and hot.

"You're lucky you didn't break your neck." He tries to make the statement scathing enough. I can tell. But perhaps he's too damn tired. The words fall flat. One could almost mistake the hitch in his voice for concern. "What the hell were you thinking?"

"Nothing. Like always."

He draws back. *Oh no.* I said the wrong thing. The naughty, spiteful, manipulative thing.

I try to take it back. "I—"

"Good morning!" A cheerful nurse appears in the doorway. "You're awake," she exclaims. "I'll get the doctor."

A man in a white lab coat comes in minutes later and spews a bunch of medical jargon while Thorny listens intently. Subdural hematoma. Stitches. Blah-dy blah. All in all, I'll be able to go home, but only if someone can monitor me overnight.

I don't even look at Thorny. Of course he'll refuse. *She'll be fine,* he'll say. *I'll come back tomorrow.*

His gaze shouldn't seek me out prior to that rejection. From this angle, his eyes are impossible to read. Like muddy pools of stagnant rain again, deceptively still.

I squirm, uneasy, as he rubs his chin and thinks.

"What do you want?" he asks finally.

My fingers are in my hair, rebelliously twisting my curls into knots. What do I want? It's a test, but I know the right words to say. "You can leave."

Frowning, he turns to the doctor. "I'll take her home."

"Excellent. I'll go over her aftercare, then."

True shock sets in as the doctor recites the warning signs Thorny should look for: dizziness, slurred speech, confusion, memory loss. I shouldn't need surgery, but just in case…

Thorny nods through his spiel. Even I'm convinced. For a second. Maybe. Then he turns to face me a second time and I can see it. That stern, serious look in his eye. How his mouth turns down into that firm Thorny frown.

On second thought, I changed my mind, he'll say.

"Maryanne," he says, deploying my name.

I shiver; it's the most devious of weapons in his arsenal.

"Do you want to come home or stay here?"

No fair. He makes it sound like a genuine question and not a trap. There's a catch, of course, waiting to be sprung the moment I fall for it. *I'll let you come home…but you'll live in the garage.*

"Do you?" he repeats.

"Yes…"

"Okay, then." He nods, taking my confession at face value. "Get dressed." He gestures to a plastic bag containing my bloody shirt and my jeans. "I'll have them draw up the paperwork."

My discharge takes hours to process. In the meantime, they run more tests, if only to be extra sure that I won't spontaneously combust. Only then am I free to go. A nurse escorts me into Thorny's car while he clambers into the driver's seat.

The door closes behind me. He starts the engine.

We start moving…

"Why?" My voice has a pathetic softness to it that I scoff to erase. Clearing my throat doesn't help any, either. I've lost my spark, along with nearly a pint of blood.

"Rest," Thorny admonishes. His fingers find the radio and switch it to classical, ensuring that the volume is low enough to keep my delicate brain from imploding. But loud enough to serve as an effective barrier.

No talking.

"Is Elaine back home?" I wonder, breaking his rule. Of course she is. *That* explains it. Elaine wanted me there, to fuss over and show what a good pseudo-mother she can be.

"No." Thorny grips the steering wheel tight, and I watch the speed gauge steadily tick higher.

"But—"

"Why did you do it?" His tone dips, matching how my stomach sinks to my toes.

Oh. So this is why he let me come back. He wanted to question me in private, away from nosy doctors and nurses.

"I'm tired." I close my eyes and press the good side of my face against the window. "My head hurts."

"Answer me." He puts in effort not to shout. I can sense it. Anger and tension prickle off him in waves regardless. He only has so much self-control.

My ass tingles beneath the denim of my jeans, and I sink deeper into my seat.

"What the hell possessed you to jump off a fucking balcony?"

"I wasn't trying to hurt myself," I admit.

He scoffs. "I know that."

Does he? I peel one eye open, but it's too dark to decipher his reaction. The shadows hide him too damn well. Only his jaw stands out in true contrast, clenched tight.

"So tell me what reason you could possibly have to—"

"You thought I was faking," I point out. He was so confident I'd been lying. An elaborate ruse of paint and makeup seemed more palatable to him than the fact that I might actually need his help.

Need *him*.

Oh no. My eyes are burning. I'm too tired. The pain pills they gave me weren't strong enough and moisture seeps from beneath my eyelids anyway. Wiping them away is my first instinct. Never let them see you cry—every good "psychopath" learned that trick. Never let them hear that telltale warble in your voice that warns of an impending sob fest.

Someone might suspect you're still human.

"Maryanne." His fingers find the radio again, switching it off. "Just..." He looks over as the glow from a passing streetlamp illuminates his face. Weathered, and stern, and fucking perfect. "Just tell me why you did it. Please."

It isn't like him to beg. I should reward him with a real juicy reply. Something he'd expect. *I knew I'd bleed. I wanted you to panic. To punish you. To taunt you.*

Everything is about you!

"I thought you locked the door," I admit. It sounds so stupid now. A laugh crawls up my throat, but it hurts to voice it. I try to choke it down. "I thought you locked the door and..."

"You thought I what?" His eyebrows furrow as he swerves to stay on the road. "Why would I... Oh." He looks away, his throat clenching around a hard swallow. "Your mother used to—"

"Because you hate me," I say over him. "Because you can't stand being alone with me. Because—"

"I don't hate you." Kudos to him. He sounds so serious for once. Not like the rehearsed speeches he's put on for my treatment team or Grandmama's benefit. *I care for Maryanne, but I don't think living with me is right for her.*

He never sounded so genuine then. Fuck him for pretending to now.

"I get it," I tell him. "I almost died. You feel guilty."

"I don't hate you." The car jerks over uneven terrain as he pulls off the main road and parks.

It's too quiet here without the noise of the engine to drown out the nuance of this moment. Our breathing. The way his fingers clutch the steering wheel so hard that the leather squeaks. How my breath fogs up the glass in little white clouds, coming faster. Faster. Faster.

"You could have fooled me." *Oops.* It's the wrong thing to say. A good girl would accept Thorny's lies hook, line, and sinker.

Caught off guard by the breach in protocol, he doesn't even have a comeback at the ready.

I should feel pleased as punch with my victory. *Hooray.* Sighing, I close my eyes. "Just take me back to the hospital—"

"I don't want to fight with you." His raised tone is a subtle warning to shut up. Let him speak. "I don't. Whatever happened to make you think… We should talk about it."

"No, thanks." Nothing says near-death experience like an impromptu trip down memory lane. I can't stop myself. I shake my head. "It doesn't matter anymore—"

"It does," he insists. "Look at me."

Touch. Soft and gentle, it tickles the hand I have braced against my knee. I jump, my heart stuttering as I try to imagine the culprit. His finger? All five of them.

"Don't touch me." Any hint of contact from him feels as fragile as a butterfly fluttering too close. You acknowledge it and *poof*—it's flown away.

"Then look at me." One shift of his palm and he's holding my hand. Without flinching. Scoffing.

My lungs stop working. I can't breathe.

"Maryanne."

I try to pull my hand away, but his latches down like a vise. That's more like it—ruthless authority with no real choice to refuse.

"Look at me."

Something in his voice tugs at that invisible leash, forcing me to glance at his stiff profile.

"I'm sorry if I hurt you," he says gruffly, his eyes fixated beyond my head. "The other day. I'm sorry."

Sorry. It's a mythical word. One I never thought I'd hear from him—ever.

My heart thumps against the inside of my rib cage, unwilling to be confined. It's too close in this car. My broken brain can't process his body heat, and his wine-tainted breath, and his touch. Not all at once.

"Please..." I wiggle my fingers, clawing at the leather seat.

This time, he lets me go.

After another minute of silence, he starts the car and we continue the rest of the way to Thornfield without another word being spoken. Thank God.

It's how we work best, Thorny and I.

By pretending the other doesn't exist.

TEN

I'm not so pretty anymore. Two rows of stitches crisscross the skin around my left eye. One stretches from my hairline down, and the other slices my cheek. A purplish bruise makes it look like my face hit more than just an errant lounger. Maybe a fist.

Thorny said I needed to be spanked. Perhaps Mother Nature heard his plea and went in a more literal direction?

She sucker-punched me.

"Maryanne?" Thorny raps on the bathroom door.

I must be taking too long. A part of me wants to take forever. Never come out.

My only solace—vocabulary word #9—is that Thorny must think I'm one hell of an Oscar-worthy makeup artist to achieve this ghoulish effect. He's waiting as I finally step into the hall.

I head for my room, but he follows behind. Too close. I hear him cross the threshold, forced to sidestep my scattered clothes. His nose wrinkles. It smells like damp clothing in here. Like must and Maryanne, the dirty little psychopath.

"I'm fine." I crawl onto my bed, freshly dressed in a clean nightgown, and lie down. There—his job is done.

But he doesn't leave. He stands there near the doorway, sucking all the air from the room and making it unbearably hot. My poor, damaged skin can't stand the heat. I scratch at it, sowing more pain in little red lines.

"You shouldn't be in my room, Daddy," I murmur into my pillow. "How scandalous. What might the neighbors think?"

"Try to get some sleep," he orders like a good general. Always observing the wounded from the front lines, but never close enough to get his hands bloody. "The doctor suggested that you shouldn't be alone for the first few hours."

And if there's anything a good, stalwart professor like Thorny can't ignore, it's doing his assigned homework.

"If I promise I won't die, will you go away?" I sneak a peek in his last direction when the silence between us has stretched beyond a minute. Then I scan the empty wall. The doorway… He left, thank God.

Or not. The broad outline of a shoulder teases my peripheral vision. He's still here.

"I don't need a babysitter."

"You're right," he says, nodding. He heads through the doorway. "I'll be back."

In the morning.

Good. I have at least eight hours of freedom from his mock concern until then. And I thought Elaine was overbearing.

Poor Thorny must be worried I might tell some nosy nurse or doctor all about the bruises on my bottom, caused by my last punishment. If I really wanted to hurt him…

Like *really* wanted to. I could always lie and say he pushed me. Hit me and came up with an elaborate ruse to cover it all up. I could. It'd be so easy.

His life is in my hands.

It's more fragile than expected—no heavier than the pink sequin pill case I snatch from my nightstand. One by one, I open each bottle and dump the required number of pills onto my pillow without bothering to lift my head. Three trazodone. One Benadryl. One Ambien. They dance over the ivory cotton like beautiful sleep-promising candies—until a big, mean hand swoops from nowhere to snatch them away.

"What are you doing?" I claw at my pill case, but it too is snatched from my reach. "Those are mine!"

"I guess someone wasn't paying attention to the doctor's instructions," Thorny grouses. Then he frowns, seeming to remember my bleeding, broken brain. His tone softens. "No sleep aids. No alcohol. No strenuous activity for at least forty-eight hours."

"But, Daddy, I need my wine and painkiller cocktail to help me sleep. It's a family tradition." I'm only half-joking. I've been prescribed medication since the age of seven. My fingers twitch, my throat empty. "They're prescription," I say, attempting to sound more serious. "Call my doctor.

They're on the up-and-up—"

"No." He shoves the case into his pocket but doesn't leave. He circles my bed instead and sits on the window seat. The horror. He's nearly within touching distance.

"What are you doing?"

He leans back, resting his head against my white wall. The silver in his hair glitters in this lighting, clashing with the gold. It makes him look dangerously shiny, lurking there. A makeshift sun in what should be a pitch-black sky. "They suggested someone stay with you overnight."

It sounds so harmless. Overnight.

"I'm fine, Daddy," I say, mumbling through my sore lip. "Peachy keen."

So get out.

"Good," Thorny says. He leans toward the light on my nightstand and switches it off. *Poof.* Darkness descends, shrouding him completely. Or not. I can still sense him there, shifting over the thin seat cushions to find a comfortable spot. "This should be an easy observation, then, and you won't have any complications from jumping headfirst off a twenty-foot balcony."

I wish.

But it's too late for that.

He is a complication, though stitches and fresh Band-Aids can't heal the damage left behind.

CROSSED LINES

*I*t's one thing to lie awake all night long. It's another to be betrayed by your own fucking blankets and the squeal of a mattress whenever you toss. Turn. Breathe.

It lets the monsters in the shadows know you're onto them. They can hear what their mere presence does to you, and you might be tempted to do something stupid in return.

Stupid like…

Throw myself off the balcony a second time. Intentionally fall down the stairs. Trip into the ocean. Hurt myself again. Hurt myself *more*.

Anything to prove he doesn't really care. I still win.

It's when the monster crawls out from under your bed that he becomes the scariest. When he takes a seat right beside you and pretends to watch you. Protect you.

Deep down, you know the truth: he's just waiting for you to fail so he can utter those terrible words. *I knew it. You were never going to change.*

The moment I wiggle to the edge of the bed and place my foot on the floor, he's upright.

"Where are you going?"

"To pee, Daddy," I say sweetly. Or at least I try to sound sweet. The painkillers are wearing off. My face feels stiff. Blinking hurts. Trying to sit up hurts. Standing requires that I cling to the canopy and use it like a rudder to find my balance.

"Be careful!" He grabs my shoulder, steering me to the door and toward the bathroom. "They said you might be uncoordinated for a few days."

But he's worried. Forty-eight hours is a deadline he's counting toward like a good uncle, waiting for the moment he can ship me right back to the ER.

Pulling away from him, I lurch into the bathroom and close the door behind me. "Does this mean no school today?" I wonder, shouting so he can hear me.

"I told Jane not to come to give you the chance to rest."

Interesting. "Oh, but I'm already so far behind, Daddy…" I trail off when I see who's staring back at me in the mirror: a monster with a bruised, bloodied face.

"You can finish up whatever work she gave you."

"So I'll be here, all alone?" I shouldn't be frowning. I *want* to be alone. So I lift the uninjured corner of my mouth as high as I can. *See? Happy face.*

"I'm working from home today," Thorny says. "I'll be in the study."

Oh. My frown returns, exaggerating my already pathetic appearance. I look so sad—that emotion an army of therapists charged my family's estate thousands to encourage me to feel. *It's okay to be sad, Maryanne,* they coached from behind reflective glasses, bundled in their pristine lab coats. *It's okay to be angry. It's okay to cry.*

It's okay to admit out loud that you've been hurt.

"I'm bleeding," I say, taking their advice. A patchwork of stitches and bandages can't stop the bright-red liquid from dripping down my cheek. I smiled too hard.

"I'm coming in."

My spine tenses as the door opens. "S-stop."

Can't he see? This room is too small for both of us. He barges in anyway, towering above as he snatches a clean washrag from the neat row on a shelf above the sink.

He wets it and dabs the blood away. Then he peels my bandages off one by one, clenching his jaw at what he sees.

"You're not supposed to show your initial horrified reaction to trauma victims," I scold. Yet another thing my therapists taught me. "You're supposed to smile and lie and tell me that everything will be all right."

"You're going to scar," he declares. My breath stills as he tilts my chin to observe me better. "But, knowing you, you'll just use each one to your benefit."

"How?" I sound too curious.

"You know how." His eyes narrow as whatever scenario he's imagining unfurls in his mind. "You'll spin some ridiculous lie as to their origin whenever it suits your needs."

Of course. Something like: *I used to be pretty, but then my crazy uncle pushed me off a balcony.*

I used to be pretty, until my uncle tried feeding me to a pack of hungry bears.

I used to be pretty. Now, I'm not. Interpret my ugly scars as you wish—just give me attention. Now. Now. Now!

"I don't want to be ugly." Weird. My voice echoes, oddly hollow. Is that what the truth sounds like?

"You're not," Thorny says, scoffing at the mere idea.

My heart squirms behind my ribs. "Really?"

"I didn't mean…" He eyes me for a second and sighs. "Let's get this over with." He finds the pack of materials the hospital sent home with me and crudely rebandages my wounds within minutes. "Come on."

Downstairs, we enter the study. He found my notebook, my pen, and the book of lessons Jane planned. They're all waiting for me, arranged in a studious row.

"I'll be down the hall if you need me," Thorny says before leaving.

If I need him.

Which I won't.

I never do.

I flip my notebook open, listening to the pages swish against the silence. I run my fingers along the lesson plan. Then I pick the pen up instead.

Jane may be my teacher, but Thorny is the world-famous super author—therefore, his assignment takes precedence.

Craft him a juicy lie worth telling.

Dear diary,

I don't think Thorny thinks of me the way an uncle should think of his niece. Sometimes I catch him staring too long. Too hard. It's like he's searching for something beneath my blouse, hidden in my skin. Dear diary, I don't know what it is.

It...

I chew on the end of my pen as I recall the rest of his advice. "Describe it."

It makes me feel...

Strange.

My skin feels hot when I know he's watching, I write. *My heart goes too fast. I can't breathe.*

Today, he touched my face when I said I was ugly. "You're not," he told me.

What does that mean?

Homework is tiring. I take a break to stare out the window. Someone rearranged the furniture on the balcony. One of the loungers is missing its cushions. There's a mop and bucket propped against the railing. He's been hard at work, Thorny.

I imagine him in his office now, writing his latest novel. About a murder, I bet. How original. Maybe the death of a young girl with an unflattering psychiatric diagnosis. She'd gotten what was coming to her, the surly old detective would deduce. Case closed.

Grandmama used to buy every novel of his on the day of release. She never read them, of course—crime thrillers were much too wild for her old-timey sensibilities. But she kept them on a shelf, lined up in a row for all to see. "My son-in-law wrote these," she'd point out to her high-class friends and assorted peons. It wasn't until after she died that I realized why. She was *proud* of him.

What a strange concept.

But, while I'm a barely literate teen with poor language comprehension, I know that Thorny hasn't published a new book in years. Ten to be exact. He's riding on the coattails of faded success.

Would Grandmama still brag about him now?

I open my notebook again and tap my pen against a fresh page. "Describe it," he instructed, my wise professor of an uncle. Add more flair.

The other day, Thorny stuck his hand up my skirt. I told him not to.

But a part of me loved feeling his palm on my ass. At least he finally wanted to touch me.

Does that make me naughty?

I close the journal and shove it aside. A throat being cleared makes me look up and jump in my seat. Thorny is standing in the doorway, conjured by my bad behavior. So perfect he is, able to sense disobedience, even if it's done in silence.

"Are you hungry?" he wonders.

"Why?" My fingers twitch, my nails tapping against the table's surface. "Are you going to feed me, Daddy?"

"What do you want?"

I fidget some more. Strange. He has yet to call me out for my use of that forbidden word. Perhaps he didn't hear me? "Something yummy, *Daddy*."

"Fine." He marches off, leaving me wondering. *Stomp. Stomp. Stomp.* His steps trail toward the kitchen.

I picture him rummaging through drawers and sniffing out whatever morsels Elaine tucked away in the fridge. When he returns an hour later, he's holding a sandwich on a plate.

His version of a watercress.

"Would you believe I'm allergic?" I ask as he places the food beside my journal. Though I can't resist fingering the spongy surface.

Unlike Elaine, he left the crusts on. And added ham. And replaced the cucumbers and watercress with a chunk of cheddar cheese.

Memory, that pesky thing, sneaks into my brain again.

"Eat," someone insisted, shoving a ham sandwich into my hands as they wiped my tears and pushed the hair back from my face. "Come on. Eat."

"I hate sandwiches," I tell him, shoving the plate aside.

"What a shame. You should get back to work, then." He grabs my journal, flipping it open to the first page.

"Hey!" My rebellious fingers try to snatch it back, but he moves to the opposite end of the room and leans across Jane's desk. As he starts to read, all I can do is shove one end of the sandwich into my mouth and bite down.

I chew mechanically as he turns the page.

Munch.

Swish.

"Better." He looks up, an eyebrow cocked. In surprise, I think. No frown, either. "Not as stiff. But you still lack the right…perspective."

I stop chewing. Try to swallow. My tongue aimlessly pushes chewed bread around my mouth, hunting for a good enough comeback. "L-like what?"

"What's my motivation?" He snaps the notebook closed, mulling it over. "Am I a sexual deviant? Or are my intentions more nefarious? 'It's like he's searching for something beneath my blouse, hidden in my skin.'" He does his best to parrot my voice and I feel my mouth wrinkle.

Do I really sound so bitchy?

"Pick up the pen."

My book lands in front of me, knocking my sandwich out of the way.

"Now, put yourself in my shoes," he commands. "What are my *intentions* when I look at you in this way? Do I want to kill you? Or do I want to corrupt you? Pick one."

"Just one?" I parrot. "Why can't it be both?"

"Because you aren't skilled enough," he snipes. "Pick."

He's too close. His creeping heat nibbles at my open pores, sneaking inside. This sensation doesn't feel thrilling enough to scribble on paper. It makes me want to crawl from the window. Away.

"I'm young and pretty," I say, meeting his gaze directly. "So of course you'd want to fuck me, *Daddy*. You're a pervert."

"Oh? Then prove it." He doesn't even flinch. His pointer finger taps the blank space beneath my neatly penned paragraphs. "Make the audience believe it. How does a person look at someone they want to fuck?"

Hmmm. Maybe they stare a little too long only to glance away when they're caught. They might bite their lower lip hard enough to punish themselves—because they know it's stupid. They know it's wrong.

But then they look again, focusing on a dangerously stern mouth. They want to make it move, even if it's into a frown. Anything.

"Oh, I don't know, Daddy," I say, folding my hands over the table. "How *does* someone look at who they want to fuck?"

A rare expression sneaks into the corner of his mouth. Part frown. Part sneer.

My lungs ram against my rib cage in protest until I remember how to suck air in again.

"You don't have much experience with the opposite sex, do you?" he asks.

"W-what?" Something inside my belly twists and squirms. He couldn't know my naughty secrets. Could he? "You said it yourself, Daddy. I'm the girl who got caught fucking a boy in the principal's office."

His name was Sammy Kean. He had rich, chocolaty hair and eyes the color of seaweed. Most days, he chewed peppermint gum too loudly and smelled like vinegar. Did he ever look at me with fuckable eyes?

No. He preferred to sneak glances at Mr. Gammer, the headmaster, when he thought no one was looking.

"You tell me," I say, turning the tables on Thorny. Before he can counter, I grab the pen and press it against his fingers. "I'm just an innocent little girl. So teach me."

His eyes flash in that stunning, hateful way. I expect him to throw the pen.

He snatches it. "Fine."

Then I watch as the nib glides across the page, forming words as it goes.

It's like his gaze is glued to my skin, tracking me. His eyes hover over my chest when I breathe, my lips when I speak.

Today, he cradled my cheek when I said I was ugly, letting his fingers linger along my jaw. "You're not," he said.

"There," Thorny declares, laying his weapon of choice down, my pride slayed. "*That* man would be labeled a pedophile."

I have to agree. This naughty uncle would be plastered all over the society pages, his career ruined, his life over.

But…

"That doesn't sound like me," I say, running my finger over the lines he wrote, smearing the ink. They look like regular old words. But they stain my skin and don't rub off when I swipe them along my skirt.

"Then dig deeper," Thorny suggests, drawing himself to his full height. "Put it in your own words."

Done teaching, he leaves.

I eat, finishing my sandwich as his words taunt me from the pages of my red journal. I tug on one, intending to tear it out. Instead, I close the book entirely.

The rest of my school day is spent brushing over Jane's lesson plan, learning nothing. When I re-enter the hallway and follow it into the living room, Thorny is already there, brooding against the mantel, his head in his hands.

"Go get ready for dinner," he commands without turning around.

"Dinner for two?" I shuffle my feet. It sounds so weird to say out loud. No Mommy to serve as a buffer between us. *Oh dear. What if we stab each other?* "Is that a good idea, Thorny? After all, you could be a lecherous pervert."

"Then I suggest you wear something decent," he says in return. "Go."

I can be a good girl when I want to be. I take my *good*, sweet time ascending the stairs, ensuring not to re-injure my battered face. I even do as he says: wear something decent. I find the perfect garment to borrow at the back of a closet.

When I enter the dining room wearing it, Thorny looks up, his eyes a mean, cold blue. Setting a wine glass down, he tucks his hand beneath his chin and watches me approach. "I always hated that dress," he declares as I linger near the doorway. "Elaine hasn't worn it in years."

Oh. I wonder why. It's flowy and practically sheer, formed of cloudy, creamy white. The modest hemline reaches below my knees. The faint hint of my pink panties can be seen through it—a fact that I try to write off as intentional, even as I shift my heels together.

Maybe it's too innocent for a man like Thorny.

"Should I take it off?" I wonder.

His eyelids lower halfway, his gaze ruthlessly focused. "Come and eat."

I sense yet another dare and can't resist skipping to the table and claiming the chair across from him. As I eye our meal, I feel my nose wrinkle. Thorny isn't like Elaine. No elaborate confections baked with care await.

Instead, he made two sandwiches on paper plates, piled high with potato chips. His plate is flanked by a glass of wine. Mine by a can of soda.

"*Bon appetit!*" I eat as slovenly—vocabulary word #12—as I can without aggravating my sore lip too badly. I let the cheese and meat dangle from between my bread slices as the latter crumbles in my grip. I lick my fingers and lazily snack on chips. *Munch. Crunch. Slurp.* Cold soda dribbles down my chin, staining Elaine's hated dress.

"Strange," Thorny muses, toying with his wine glass. His eyes perform a slow trip up and down my face and my torso. He lingers near my neck, and I shift, pressing my knees together. "I'm sure your grandmother taught you table manners."

"Haven't you heard?" I lick the salt off a chip and noisily chew it.

He doesn't bother to return my beautiful smile. So serious.

"I grew up in a barn. It was called 'boarding school.' My mean uncle shipped me off to twelve of them and the only manners I learned were how many ways to say 'abandonment issues' in group therapy."

He frowns. Takes a sip of wine. Another.

"And," I add, continuing my tale. Just for funsies. "You want to know the best part? I've been to twelve schools, but he never ever let me go to his. The fancy, exclusive one he teaches at, you see? I think it's called Waldo? Weirdo?"

"Be honest," Thorny softly chides. "Why would you even want to go to Walden?"

The truth? "Maybe I just wanted to learn from you, Daddy? Maybe I wanted to see what it's like to have your undivided attention."

That makes him frown more deeply as he drains his wine glass. "Eat."

We do, and when we finish, I head up to my room while he lurks downstairs. I can hear him pacing circles. Talking?

To Elaine, I suspect, on the phone.

"She's fine," he growls. "I said she's fine. You know what… Stop! Just *stop*. Don't call me for now. Give me time—stop with the fucking excuses! I don't want to hear it."

He hangs up. Paces some more.

Tracking his every movement, I crawl into bed, only to remember he still has my pill case. When he marches up the stairs, he doesn't enter my room though. He keeps going, moving slower the farther down the hall he ventures. Until he stops right near where I suspect the threshold of his bedroom to be.

I lie here beneath the blankets, listening to the floor creak beneath the weight of his indecision. Back and forth. Forth and back.

Eventually, he turns and marches down the stairs, storming deeper into the house.

He's like thunder, Thorny. He can't help that he's a herald for something wild and out of control, or that the storm in his wake destroys everything in its path. His only course of action is to rumble through the chaos, slamming doors and snatching wine bottles from his study.

The sandwich was just a snack for him. Alcohol is his real sustenance. He'll drink it all night, the same way my ears subsist on seeking out every faint sound he makes, just to be sure he's really here. He hasn't left.

We're greedy with our vices, gobbling them up whole. It's the only way we know how to cope.

TWELVE

I wake up too early. There's a bad dream in my head, chasing me into the hallway. I have to run to escape it, right into a bedroom, its closet doors left wide open.

But this one is dark. Empty.

The only other occupant of the house lurks outside it, brooding on the balcony below. He's staring into a wine bottle as moonlight reflects off the waves in the distance. As I tiptoe closer, he looks up, spotting me.

This is a dream. Therefore, it's okay for my stomach to dip as I grasp the banister. He observes me with more interest than he ever would in reality, swiping his thumb along his jaw to whisk wine away. Anticipation builds as curiosity lingers in his irises. He'll ask me something, I think. One of those dangerous questions only he can pose.

But... Like always, he turns away and ignores me instead.

I bet he's thinking up a new plot idea. Something cerebral and enthralling, involving a cheating wife and a single father with a mean, rebellious daughter. Sometimes they pretend to be happy families. Sometimes not.

And, in the end, everyone dies.

I copy him, thinking hard. What layer might I add to my own sordid fairytale?

"Thorny?" *Oops.* I break the spell, calling down to him directly.

He shrugs, but I don't expect him to respond—not really. I think I imagine the gruff words riding a gust of wind.

"What do you want?"

"Your book. *Wasteland—*"

His shoulders stiffen at the title of his debut novel. From shock? I can't tell.

Swallowing hard, I add, "Why did the woman fake her own death?"

A rather anticlimactic ending, if I do say so myself. The detective hero spent years chasing the murdered heiress only to find her living quietly as someone else.

"You read it?" Thorny looks at me sharply.

My shoulders lift in a shrug. "Ages ago."

A lie. There's a dogeared copy hidden at the very bottom of my suitcase. One of many paperbacks with his name stamped on them. For research purposes and nothing more. How can I get under his skin without getting inside his head first?

My uncle Thorny has a devious, dark mind.

"Because." He stares back at the water, his reply so soft that I have to strain my ears to catch it. "She wanted to know what it felt like."

"To what?" I wonder, leaning against the railing, so close to slipping off again.

"To disappear." Something he does now, darting beneath the balcony and out of my reach.

The next morning, Thorny is waiting for me in the study. The air feels different the moment I enter the room. Close and still, like we're sharing every inhaled breath. He doesn't look at me—not yet. Still, I feel his attention seep into every little pore.

"Morning," he says in a tone dripping with nonchalance.

"No Jane?" I question after licking my dry lips.

"Not today…" He looks up from a pile of paperwork, eyeing me strangely.

My fingers twitch, aching to cover my cheek, but I stop myself. I took the bandages off, letting my wounds air out in the bright, happy sunshine.

"It doesn't look too bad," he says finally. "Maybe you won't scar too badly after all."

My eyes bulge. Was that a compliment?

"Your lessons will resume tomorrow," he adds, returning his attention to his documents. "You can continue with whatever work she left."

I sit at the table and open my journal. Like a dutiful student, I jot down a few lines. Then I pause.

Thorny remains in the corner, steadily working away.

Odd.

We're in the same room. Doesn't he realize?

I listen to the scratch, scratch of his pen as it crawls across the page. Tentatively, I copy the motion with a few scribbles of my own.

I caught him watching me last night. In the dark when he thought I wasn't looking. I shouldn't have worn that nightgown, the old one that's far too thin. You can see my nipples through it.

Did he?

I look up, glancing at Thorny. Then I scratch out the last few lines and try again.

Last night, I wore my thinnest nightgown, telling myself he wouldn't stare. It's wrong. He's my uncle. Even if it's thin enough to see through.

He'd look away...

"Let's see it." Thorny shoves his work aside and holds out his hand expectantly.

"Huh?" I blink, batting my eyelashes. "See what?" My fingers flutter over my words, shielding them from view.

"Don't tell me you're suddenly shy." He stands and four quick strides bring him to me. When he extends his hand again, I have no choice but to surrender the journal. "Not bad," he declares after reading the first few lines. "Decent word choice."

"R-really?" My stomach clenches as he continues to read.

"Yes. Your phrasing has improved. But…what are the stakes?" He shrugs and slams my book shut. "What is at risk if your lecherous uncle crosses the line?"

He leans in. Way too close. My nostrils flare to inhale him, and I wiggle against the back of my seat, trapped by wood and leather.

"Dig deeper, Maryanne," he scolds, tsking between his teeth. "Make me feel the risk."

He picks up my pen and hands it to me. So I try again.

He's married, I write. My hand stills as he circles the table and reads from over my shoulder.

"Keep going," he commands.

He's married, I scrawl obediently. *And Elaine loves him so, so much. If she saw the way he looked at me, she'd—*

"Enough." His expression clouds over and darkens as he steps back.

Oops. We're not playing anymore. I bent the rules too far, and he's packing up his toys, leaving the room.

"W-wait," I say, even though he's already in the living room, sliding the glass doors to the balcony open. "I didn't mean it."

But it's too late. Second chances are for good girls.

He avoids me for the rest of the day, exiting whatever room I enter or lingering on the balcony. The only way to watch him is to sneak glimpses from the master bedroom, crouched on all fours, just beyond his line of sight.

A wild Thorny in his natural habitat is a strange creature to behold. He takes a drink. Sighs. Takes another drink. His eyes scan the water ruthlessly, and I remember something Elaine said: "He hates going down to the beach." Except, of course, in the early morning hours after his wife left him.

Can wise, old Thorny not swim? No. I bet there's more to it than that. Something complicated, befitting a man with such a creative mind.

I bet he hates sand. It's unruly, unable to be tamed. Like a wayward teenage psychopath, it gets into places it shouldn't, chafing against the desired order.

Yeah. That's it. How fucking pretentious.

I watch him until the sunlight fades and he returns inside, his bottle empty. Through the floor, I sense the sliding glass door slam shut.

"Maryanne!"

"Coming!" I scoot back into the master bedroom, taking care not to leave a clue I was ever there. When I race down the stairs, he's in the dining room. There are four sandwiches this time.

"Eat," he grunts, biting into his first one.

I linger near the edge of the table, flicking imaginary crumbs off its surface. He's halfway through his second sandwich when I finally gather up the nerve to speak.

"What does it feel like to write?"

He spends hours avoiding it. It must be fun.

"What?" He eyes me above his mound of bread. "Are you serious?"

"Maybe." I pick a seat and claim a sandwich. My nostrils flare, catching his scent. *Oopsies.* I'm two chairs closer than before. "So what does it feel like? Playing make-believe and getting paid. Didn't your mommy ever encourage you to get a real job?"

The fact that he does have one is beside the point.

"Tell me what it's like to tell lies for a living," I dare him.

"It's fulfilling," he says. "Something you wouldn't understand."

"Because I'm so 'crazy'?" I make air quotes.

He laughs, and I catch myself staring. It almost sounded real.

"No," he says, remembering his customary scowl. "Because it requires putting yourself in someone else's point of view and thinking from a different angle. It requires a *lack* of selfishness."

"Oh." I poke my sandwich with my thumb. "So tell me, if I were to put myself in the shoes of, say, a middle-aged man in a perfect marriage, why might my wife want to leave me?"

"Fucking hell..." He jolts upright, knocking his wine glass over. The dark liquid spreads across the table, dripping onto my lap. There goes my favorite skirt.

"Don't," I blurt when he heads for the door. But my mouth wrinkles. Sarcasm should be delivered guilt-free. Maybe I wasn't using it that time. "I...I didn't mean it like that."

"Oh." He releases an exaggerated sigh and rocks back onto his heels. "And how did you fucking mean it?"

"I... No one's ever loved me." I make it sound so matter-of-fact. Common knowledge. "I'm curious. Researching and all."

He scoffs, shooting me a disgusted glance. "Is that what you go around saying to justify your behavior?"

"Put yourself in my shoes." I tap my fingers against the table. It's story time, but I'm nowhere near as good at it as he is. "*You* are a seventeen-year-old girl dumped from boarding school to boarding school. Your own family wants nothing to do with you—"

"And whose fault is that?" His voice rises.

Mine grows softer, though I'm not sure why. "So you get sent to live with your aunt and uncle who pretend to have the world's best marriage. But it's a lie."

"Everything is a joke to you, isn't it?" He fumes, radiating tension. For whatever reason, though, he doesn't leave. No. He shoves a chair away from the table and perches on the end of it. Both hands clasped, he faces me coldly. Class is now in session. "If I were that girl, maybe I'd stop to wonder just what about me makes people—"

"Hate?" I say, venturing a guess like a good student.

He grits his teeth. "Avoid."

"Ah." I nod along. "And if you were that girl and the *one* person in the world to show you any ounce of kindness when you needed it the most throws you away like garbage. What might you think?"

Oops. It's the wrong thing to say. Truthful bile, vomited up uncontrollably.

"And what might you think if he picked at you constantly," I add, weaving my tale as best I can. "And he *lived* for finding something nefarious—a new vocabulary word, by the way—in every little thing you do, what might you think then?" I lurch to my feet, knocking my chair over in the process. The room is spinning. My face is burning. My eyes are leaking. "If you were that girl, would you know what love is?"

"Maryanne—"

"No! You wouldn't," I say, copying his smug, all-knowing tone. "Because every time you showed an ounce of it to anyone they disappear, or hang themselves, or *leave!*"

I don't run to my room—I walk quickly. He didn't get to me. No. I'm fine. It's all an act—everything I do, think, and feel is an act. I'm not entitled to portray real emotions.

I'm too damn manipulative.

"Maryanne!"

He sounds closer than he should be. When I turn to slam the door, he's behind it, his expression a stranger's. Wide-eyed. Worried. Concerned?

"Haha," I call thickly, slumped against the wood. "I got you!"

The doorknob jiggles, but I lock it before it can turn.

"Maryanne…"

"*Lala, I can't hear you!*" My hands crush my ears, blocking him out.

He doesn't stay long. He doesn't even knock again. One second. Two.

He's gone.

THIRTEEN

*M*orning is a reset button. So I skip downstairs wearing an enormous smile, my hair in pigtails. Nothing I say ever matters for long. I'm fickle like that. Therefore, Thorny shouldn't be waiting for me at the bottom of the steps.

"Here." He shoves a bundle into my arms the moment I'm close enough and jerks his chin in the direction I came from. "Get dressed. Then meet me in the car."

Ah. My smile falls flat. My hands loosen their grip, sending whatever he gave me toppling to the floor.

Over a week. I lasted that long. Just long enough to forget for a second that I was always on borrowed time.

Touché, Thorny. He's won the war.

"Did you hear me?" He looks up, unaffected by my shocked expression. "Hurry up." He smooths his hand along the crisp tan suit I notice for the first time. "We're going to be late."

Late? Mr. Lawyer gets paid by the hour. A few extra dollars won't kill him.

But…

Visits to his office don't typically require a dress code. I sweep my gaze over the discarded garments scattered over the steps and my eyes widen. A blue-and-yellow-plaid skirt. A navy sweater with a golden crest emblazoned over the left breast. When I seek him out, I have to swallow to keep my voice steady.

"You're taking me to Walden?"

I wait for him to scoff. Haha. I fell for his nasty trick.

"Hurry up," he snaps, marching through the front door. "You have five minutes."

Five minutes. It takes me three to run upstairs, change, and race out to the car. Thorny says nothing before pulling off, his expression even more closed off than usual. Usually, I'd poke and prod him to find out why, but I'm too busy bouncing in my seat. The fields and beaches of Thornfield fade, and almost comically close by, the landscape surrenders to neat, polished school grounds.

Walden is a stone structure built like a castle, rising from the crest of a hill, overlooking a different view of the ocean. All this time, it was only about an hour's walk away.

"Stay close," Thorny warns as he parks near the main building. Several outposts, draped in ivy, make it feel like a collection of neat stone blocks arranged around a central courtyard. "You're still under observation," he says.

Oh. I swipe my hand over my bandaged face. This is why he brought me; my busted brain means he can't leave me alone.

"You are to sit at the back of my class. The moment you step out of line, you're on your way home. Understood?"

I bite my tongue and nod. There's no point in risking his ire —vocabulary word #19—now. I follow him diligently across the campus and into the main building as students dressed in uniform mill about.

It reminds me of the good old days. When I was the one skulking around the edges of the populace, going unnoticed while clamoring for attention in the same conflicted breath. Teenage girls are strange creatures. Thorny navigates them with stiff shoulders and a frown that warns he can't be fucked with.

I would have made a point of provoking him though. Just because. He has that kind of face. The overtly handsome one you want staring in your direction, focused on you always.

Even if he's angry.

Especially when he's angry.

His classroom is on the second floor with a view of the water. How fitting for someone who likes to drink himself into a stupor while staring at the ocean. I wonder if there's vodka in the mug he sets on his desk.

At least ten girls are already seated, giggling in anticipation of his arrival. They send me curious looks, but Thorny makes for a more interesting target. They can barely take their eyes off him.

"This is Maryanne," he explains while settling behind the desk at the head of the room. The sharp jerk of his chin directs me to the desk in the very last row, far outside the influence of his delicate flock.

His students watch him like sheep would a wolf. The dumb, innocent kind of sheep from children's fables. He's dressed to kill, his eyes sharp, seeking out the hint of wandering attention. When he's sure he has them rapt and at the ready, he turns to the chalkboard.

"Today, our topic is…sex."

The class gasps aloud as he writes the naughty word for all to see in white chalk. My mouth may be open too. I run my thumb along my lower lip to check. It's wet and my tongue traces it as those three letters appear on the blackboard.

SEX

"Primarily, the role of sex in literature," he continues, lest someone get any naughty ideas. "Men and women play different character tropes in many novels. Anyone care to name a few?"

A ruddy-faced girl with bright-red hair raises her hand and beams when called upon. "The man is the protector, like a knight," she says. "While the lady is always the princess. The one in danger."

"Or," Thorny adds while writing her response across the chalkboard, "the temptress. Anyone remember the story of Adam and Eve?"

His students giggle and throw out more boring clichés.

The witch and the warlock.

The wicked husband and the dutiful wife.

When I raise my hand, I sense him deliberately pass over me more than once. He calls on another blond instead.

"Women usually are in the background, while the man is the lead," she says.

"Right." Thorny nods and adds that to the bottom of his growing list. "And—"

"The innocent little girl and the big, bad wolf," I say, breaking protocol.

Thorny stiffens midsentence. His shoulders ripple as he sets the chalk aside and turns around. My stomach clenches in anticipation of his reaction. *Odd.* He's thoughtful, appraising me with his head cocked to the side.

"Or predator and prey," he says, rephrasing my words. "A common trope."

"Is it though?" I shrug. "Maybe not. Little Red Riding Hood was wearing *red.* What if she knew that was the wolf's favorite color?" I lean across my desk, focused on Thorny even as the other students turn to stare. "What if... she wanted to get eaten up from the very beginning?"

"Interesting take," Thorny deadpans. "In fact, that's the perspective I want you all to adopt."

His change in tone must be a familiar cue. In unison, his students fish through the bookbags propped against the chairs and withdraw notebooks and pens. It's study time.

"Today's lesson is to invert those preconceived notions you have. Take whatever trope you feel is the most familiar and turn it on its head. Reverse the sexes."

Like lambs to the slaughter, his students dive headfirst into the assignment, hunched over their desks, intent with concentration.

"Here." A stack of clean paper and a silver pen land before me.

Invert a cliché and make it my own. I nibble on the end of my pen as I watch the other students hard at work. I bet Thorny loves this: having power over little girls who bow to his authority. They don't talk back.

They don't push his buttons.

They don't challenge those "preconceived" notions floating around his distinguished brain.

The class is nearly over by the time I finally scribble something down. I glance up without realizing it, meeting his gaze as he observes the class from the head of the room. He raises an eyebrow.

What are you up to? I imagine him thinking.

I smile a smile just for him and keep writing. But it's a twisted game of my brain spouting nonsense and my hand racing to scratch it out and start over. By the time I compose the semblance of a paragraph, Thorny rises to his feet.

"Class dismissed."

Muttering amongst themselves, his students race out single-file, eager for their next class.

But not me. He'll only give me a taste, nothing more.

Looking at me, he nods to the doorway. "Let's go."

Resigned, I follow him back to the car, saying nothing. During the drive over to Thornfield, I can't help thinking that it might be better to starve.

At least then you don't know what you're missing.

"I have another class to teach," Thorny tells me, pulling up to the front of the house. "You'll be all right on your own for a few hours." He hesitates, and I suspect those words were directed at himself more than at me. "Stay out of trouble. Finish your assignment."

My assignment. I retreat to my bedroom and smuggle my red journal beneath the covers. Invert expectations, Thorny said. Destroy all preconceived notions.

Tell a lie worth telling.

Dear diary,

It makes me feel so pathetic, wanting him to want me. It's such a stupid wish. No, desire might be a better word. I'm seven again every time he looks at me.

That's all he sees. A worthless burden he didn't want.

But he was all I needed. All I wanted.

You can crave a hug from someone so much it hurts. You can claw at their fingers, begging them to open, even as they walk away. You can scream and shout, but they ignore you.

They run from you.

So you run toward them. And you shout louder, and you kick harder, and you scream ten times higher.

It's the only way to get their attention.

But the person they see isn't really you. It's just a mask.

And they despise you for wearing it.

But the really sad part? You can't remember how to take it off.

Reading over the scribbled sentences, I laugh out loud. Haha. It's such a whiny confession that Thorny would never believe it came from me. Such stupid, bleating, pointless bitching. I rip it out and ball it up before letting it bounce across my floor.

My eyes are burning because it's late. I haven't slept well in three days—since he stole my pills. The moisture seeping down my cheeks is just a trick of the breeze blowing through my window, cooling my skin.

Nothing more.

Thorny gets back when it's dark outside and I've already stuffed my face with a sandwich crudely made from the last bit of deli meat in the fridge. He enters the house silently, a cell phone pressed to his ear. Without looking at me once, he heads straight for the balcony, leaving the glass door open so that his words trickle in.

"I don't want to 'talk about this later,'" he growls. "Say it now. Fuck! Say it now!"

I jump. He's never shouted like this before. So loud that I feel it vibrating in my bones, which makes them quiver. My knees draw together, my stomach a twitching, nervous thing.

"You think I haven't fucking known? All this time? That I don't fucking know!"

Elaine must say something pleading in that soft, soothing voice of hers. *Please.*

Whatever it is makes Thorny laugh. "Fuck him. How long have you been screwing him, huh? Before or after that piece of shit stole my manuscript? Don't pretend like you don't fucking know—"

He lowers the phone from his ear, letting the wind swallow up Elaine's reply.

"Fuck you," Thorny rasps when she goes silent. "Fuck the both of you."

He hurtles the phone. It strikes the house, ricocheting off and sliding beneath a lounger. Sighing, he leans against the railing, clutching his head in his hands.

"Fuck," he hisses to no one. "Fuck! Fuck! *Wait*—"

I look down, surprised to find that I'm on my feet, inches from the hallway. Like a dog on a leash, I jerk in place. Frozen.

"Come here." He has his back to me, but he beckons with a wave of his hand.

Uh-oh. I'm so used to him pushing me away. I don't know how to react when he draws me closer. My feet twitch, my brain going blank. Cautiously, I take a step toward the balcony. Then another.

A cool breeze nips at my skin, warning me away the closer I come. He's inverted expectations. The tables have turned. Giving in will only strengthen the inevitable sting when he rips the proverbial rug from beneath me.

But I've always been a glutton for his brand of punishment. Silence and lies. Interest only when I start to believe he'll never show it.

It's addictive whiplash.

"I want to ask you something," he confesses, his shoulders hunched, his gaze on the horizon.

"Yes?"

"Your mother. Why did she leave?"

My chest constricts as the blood in my body drains back to my heart. It's the taboo subject of which we never speak.

My mother, the original blond-haired, blue-eyed psychopath. The woman who gave birth to me on a whim and skipped out when I was barely seven. The vengeful love interest who drove my father to suicide.

"She left," I say. The same thing I recite to the many therapists, teachers, and psychiatrists who've asked the same question. Marie got bored. She returned to France.

Marie started a new family after relinquishing her parental rights over me as soon as she could.

Marie was a bitch.

"She abandoned you," Thorny says, using the mean word my therapy sessions discouraged.

Marie "got overwhelmed with life." It wasn't about me or my father. Deep down, she probably loved us both very much. Probably.

"Why?" he demands. "Did he cheat on her? Screw some other woman? Did you throw one of your fucking little tantrums and drive her away? Why?"

"She just left." I sound hollow. A terrible actress reciting the only line I remember from the terrible play I'm in: *The Life of Maryanne Mayweather.* "She just—"

"Left," he snarls. "In the middle of the fucking day. With no goddamn reason." He forms a fist and slams it against the railing. "No. There *had* to be a fucking reason. So, what did you do?"

He bellows the question, demanding an answer.

What did I do?

"I…"

I wanted her to love me.

I begged her to stay.

I wanted her to need me. Keep me. Please. Pleasepleaseplease! I wanted to be better and perfect and smile and be good.

I promised to be good.

It didn't matter.

"I existed," I hear myself say. "It wasn't my fault."

"No. *You* drove her away," he deduces, smiling coldly at the realization. *Aha!* He cracked the code that had evaded my father. "You drive everyone the fuck away. Do you want to know why?"

My heart thumps, beating and exposed. His words are a rusty knife, aimed without care. He just wants to hurt. To make me bleed.

"Because you're so fucking desperate for attention. No one else gave you the time of fucking day and I knew you'd bleed me dry. You bleed everyone fucking dry."

I blink as my hands claw at each other, pinching and scratching. It hurts, but not enough to help me ignore the pain slicing beneath my rib cage, spreading like blood. The air in my lungs seeps out along with it. Drip. Drop. I'm hemorrhaging.

"Are you listening to me?" He grabs my chin, tilting my face closer. We're eye to eye now. His are bloodshot and unfocused. Alcohol drips from his breath, seeping into me.

I sway. Maybe this is secondhand intoxication?

"You're pathetic," he hisses. "You use people like tools. You think you really win them over—but it's a lie. They could never love you in the first fucking place—" He breaks off, frowning as his thumb grazes my cheek and comes away wet. "Is this how you fooled the others? You cried on command?"

He's referring to his sisters. My family. Their friends. How I charmed and manipulated them, twisting my emotions to suit whatever fit the occasion.

I'm a master manipulator.

Feelings? I have no feelings.

I'm not crying now. Crying is fake. You boo-hoo and pinch your wrist until your eyes water. *Ta-da!* The person tormenting you feels guilty and you live another day.

I'm not crying. My boo-hoos aren't rehearsed and dainty. My throat makes a weird noise and I try to hide my face. Smother my mouth with my hands. Anything to shut up.

I sound like a cat that broke its leg once. The damn thing couldn't stop wailing. Whimpering. It wailed and wailed and wailed. It curled up in a little ball and screamed when I tried to touch it.

Crying is for Daddy's funerals and Mommy's unapologetic goodbyes.

The real pain comes when you're alone. When your heart rips from your chest, bleeds out of your eyes, and you can't catch your breath. You can't sniffle and peek through your lashes to watch the sucker you're conning fall for it.

You shriek like a helpless little kitten.

"Maryanne… I'm sorry. *I'm sorry.*"

The wood of the balcony chafes my knees. I'm clinging to the railing with one hand, hiding my face with the other. Something heavy weighs me down, unbearably warm. It shudders as I struggle to breathe, growling insistently into my ear.

"I'm sorry," he says. "It's me! It's fucking *me*. Everyone always leaves me. I'm sorry. I'm such a fucking…"

I'm suffocating, wrapped up tight by two arms, strong and firm, that crush me to a heavier body hunched over mine.

"I'm sorry. Do you hear me?" He rakes the hair from my eyes with shaking fingers, burying his face against my neck. "It's me, not you. *I'm* the fucked-up one…"

The one who runs.

Who leaves.

The one who drives everyone away.

Morning is a reset button—but this time, the universe doesn't hit it properly. I wake up smelling salty air, with the sun beating down on my skin.

Something heavy and warm shrouds me from most of the vengeful rays though. An arm. A shoulder. A body nearly twice as long as mine.

He smells the way I assume older men smell. Like wine, and sea salt, and stale cologne. He's awake. I know it from how he's breathing: raggedly and slowly. Like each intake of air requires that he manually churn it down his throat and through his lungs.

Because every drop of oxygen is tainted with me and he's too sober to deal.

I sneak a peek through a crack in my eyelids. We're too close, Thorny and I. More than touching. *Clinging.* My head is resting against his shoulder, and I can see the blondish stubble coating his jaw when I look up. He's brooding, his teeth clenched tight, his eyes narrowed and stormy.

I could be dreaming. I try to pinch myself just to be sure, but his posture shifts slightly.

Poof. The spell is broken.

His arm tenses around me then goes slack. I should do the polite thing and scoot away, maintaining our distance.

But I don't. I linger guiltily while his heartbeat plays a frantic tune that melds with the crash of the ocean's waves.

Swish. Thump. Swish.

"We need to talk," he says. I can hear the words form in his chest and croak from his throat, but they sound so heavy. So tired.

Talk. I know about what.

"Wait." He grabs me when I try to stand.

Rejection is a pill best swallowed on your feet. Ideally after, you can hide for a few hours and reassemble your armor of charming grins and carefree giggles.

Tired, with tangled hair and sore skin—I'm not strong enough.

"You can send me away later," I blurt out. God, I'm pleading. "But just don't—"

"I'm not sending you away. Come here." Thorny sighs and tugs me down, forcing me to crouch.

We're on the same level now. It's strange down here. If I squint, it almost seems like he's not leaning away from me.

"Go get dressed," he says, compiling a new plan on the fly. "We'll...we'll go for a drive."

A drive. To Mr. Lawyer's stuffy office?

Thorny rises without an explanation, still wearing his rumpled teacher ensemble, his hair a wild mess. "I'll be in the car," he grumbles before lumbering through the house, ever the storm cloud.

Like a good girl, I heed his command. I go upstairs and shower. Then I get dressed in my last clean sweater and another pair of jeans. I've run out of clean clothes: four weeks of clothing is all I've ever really needed.

When I return downstairs, I half-expect to find the driveway empty. He'll take his drive alone, clear his head, and fix whatever malfunction made him say those dangerous words in the first place.

I'm sorry.

It's me.

I'm the fucked-up one.

I approach the front door cautiously and open it. It's bright outside. The sun beams off a cherry-red convertible, almost as if taunting me. He's seated behind the steering wheel, staring resolutely at the windshield.

When I descend the front steps, he doesn't drive off.

Odd.

He doesn't frown, either, when I slip into the passenger's seat and close the door behind me. Instead, he sighs that tired way only he can. Then he rolls our windows down and flicks the radio on.

Classical music can be an effective barrier. It seeps into the silence and gives it depth—something anyone wishing to break it has to fight to overcome. He uses the music to keep me at bay, and I watch the world pass from behind the window rather than fight.

He's taking me into town. The closer we come to Thornton, the more my stomach tenses, feels queasy. When we pass buildings and street signs near Mr. Lawyer's office, I'm not surprised. A good, brave girl would face the bitter end and smile.

Fuck everyone.

No one can reject me.

I've rejected them first.

But I was prettier then. And whole. And maybe a little less tired from having slept in a real bed and not in Thorny's arms.

That's the mean part: He *let* me sleep there. He lied to me. He pretended, even for a second, that the obvious wasn't in store.

The car comes to a stop before an intersection and I shrug my seat belt off. The door opens with little resistance. *Voila.* I'm free, skipping out of the path of an oncoming truck.

"What the hell are you doing?" Thorny shouts over furious honking.

What am I doing?

I set my sights on the first destination I find. "I'm going shopping," I say over my shoulder. "I need new clothes."

Clothing fit enough to be thrown away in. Something made of sequins, gaudy and blinding. Thorny is old. I could always blame his not wanting me on his poor, poor eyes: I'm far too much for them to handle on a daily basis.

Not that this boutique has much that catches my interest. It's small, with frilly lace things. The clothing displayed in the window looks like the horrifying cross between something one might find in Elaine's closet and Grandmama's. Beautiful, expensive, and plain.

I enter through a small doorway with a chiming bell and finger the first thing I cross: a seafoam-green dress with a stuffy silhouette.

"Hello!" The lone saleswoman flashes a beaming grin in my direction. Then her eyes widen, fixated on someone barreling into the store after me.

I can't resist sneaking a peek. Thorny huffs and puffs his way past a carousel of clothing. In the unflattering daylight, he looks even more disheveled. Before he can say a word, I snatch up a dress in a hideous shade of yellow and hold it against my chest.

"Think this would make me look pretty?"

His eyes narrow as his lips twitch to deliver his trademark rebuttal. *Enough, Maryanne!* "I don't know," he says dispassionately. "Try it on."

Uh-oh. I recognize a dare when I hear it. I set the yellow dress aside and pick out an even simpler one of gray silk and white lace. "This one?" I finger the hem thoughtfully. "Think it will make me look grown up?"

"No." He holds my gaze and points to a mannequin posed near the back of the store. "Try that one."

It's a paisley-patterned sundress—red, white, and yellow. Not quite Elaine. Not quite Maryanne, the chaotic mess of a girl. It's different, and my stomach clenches in warning.

But a dare's a dare.

"Fine."

I take the dress into the dressing room and pull it on over my sweater and my pants. There. I stick my tongue out at my reflection.

If I squint, I can almost pretend it's not me. Someone new, maybe? Someone who wouldn't be driven to the proverbial dump the moment she said boo.

This time, it wasn't even my fault.

Haha. I scowl at my reflection. *Are those tears?*

Of course not.

I swipe my hand across my wounded cheek and then step outside, smiling so hard that my mouth aches. "Tada!" I hold my arms out and twirl. But I can't complete a full circle without sneaking another glimpse at his face, ready to gloat over the scowl that I know is plastered there.

But his face is blank—alarmingly so. His eyes reflect nothing as he watches the fabric swish and dance around my legs. Up they travel, tracing the bulky contours of the satin stretched over my clothing. My hips. Waist. Quivering throat.

"It's a bit too mature for you," he says, meeting my gaze.

It's not the word itself that makes my cheeks heat up and sting. It's how he says it. *Too* mature.

"Take it off and let's go."

I hover near the mouth of the dressing room, teased by the reflection lurking from the corner of my eye. My fingers seize a handful of fabric and won't let go. "I...I want it."

He grits his teeth in that impatient way. "We don't have time to—"

"Please?"

He stares at me and then glowers at his watch. "Fine." His hand sneaks into his back pocket and removes a wallet. He fishes out a crisp bill and hands it to the saleswoman.

"Car," he commands me after. The bell chimes as he exits while the saleswoman packs my dress in a nest of tissue paper and seals the entire package in a white shopping bag.

The victor takes the true spoils of war, but at least, this time, I get a souvenir in addition to my battle wounds. Something to reflect upon one day, if I ever feel bored enough, on all the ways I'll never measure up to Thorny's lofty expectations.

He likes muted colors and crisp, clean lines. He likes to play Mozart as he drops off wayward family members. He likes to take the long way there, winding through town, drawing the inevitable out.

Until he leaves town altogether.

As Thornton fades in the distance, I sit straighter in my seat, scouring our surroundings with renewed interest. We're on the west side of the island now. Where the neat, picket-fenced parish gives way to grassy knolls and windswept beaches. It's the rocky, forsaken wilds that tourists avoid and locals creep only to remind themselves how good they have it on their privately maintained lands.

Thorny drives up a winding road, following the coast. For hours, it feels like, but the sun stubbornly doesn't seem to move from its spot in the sky. As the ocean eats up more and more land, he switches Mozart off.

"We bring out the worst in each other, you know." He makes it sound like some novel concept he just discovered. The worst in him equates to scowls, and glares, and mean, nasty words.

The worst in me? Naughty sarcasm and fingers quick to push his buttons. Poke. Poke. It's so easy to make him roar sometimes. It's so easy to make him shout, and turn red, and stomp around like a living thunderstorm.

I've never made him talk though. And it's the worst. He has no polished filter, like this.

He means every word he says. Words tipped like arrows, aimed mercilessly.

"We really do…" He sighs and eyes the gray sky as though it might be able to tell him why. "But I can't live like this. I refuse to. So let it out."

He waves his hand to put weight behind the command. *Speak.*

"Say whatever it is you've been holding on to all these years. Let's put it all out into the open once and for all. Say it."

My arms crisscross over my chest. "I'm not sure what you mean, Daddy."

"Oh?" He holds his palm out as if to feed my words back to me. *Aha!* Exhibit A. "We could start with why you call me 'daddy' when you know it—" He grits his teeth, holding the bad words back.

When you know it drives me fucking insane?

"You know what? Fuck it." He takes his own advice. "You *know* it pisses me off. It makes me feel like a goddamn pervert. So why say it?"

Why? I mull it over. "Maybe I like making you angry."

"Of course." Thorny scoffs, shaking his head. He flicks the radio on, switching it to full volume. "I should have known," he hisses above the melody. "You can't be serious for one fucking—"

"Maybe it's the only way you hear me."

To prove me wrong, Mozart cuts off and the silence returns, too loud to smother. I have to chip away at it with tiny breaths. When that doesn't work, my fingers scratch at the leather of my seat. *Scritch. Hiss.*

"Go on," Thorny demands. His hollow tone is a wrecking ball.

Suddenly, everything is noise; my heart plays a violent melody as my teeth hammer the accompanying percussion. "Calling you Daddy," I admit in a rush. "Maybe it's the only way you ever respond to me."

"That's ridiculous." He shakes his head, his lips drawn tight over his gnashing teeth. "Be serious—"

"I *am*."

And that's the sad part. I'm honest and he sneers down his nose and orders me to stop. I lie and he flies into a rage. But at least then he looks at me. Really looks.

It doesn't matter if he doesn't like what he sees.

At least I know I'm still here.

"You can never just be upfront about something." He sounds so overwhelmed, Thorny. Poor him. He's the one whose entire life has been on puppet strings, manipulated by guardian after guardian. *He's* the one who gets balled up and thrown away like scribbled journal pages.

Poor James Thorne—he's the victim.

"Where are you going?"

My hand is on the door handle again, shoving it open. I place one foot on the damp sand edging the road. A stretch of beach is only a few paces away. Plenty of space. I need space. My chest feels too tight. I'm breathing too fast.

When I climb out of the car, Thorny slams his fist over the horn, blaring it. *BEEEP!*

"For fuck's sake, Maryanne! I try to talk to you like an adult and you can't even—"

"Daddy," I say, watching him sputter, enraged into silence. "Daddy. Daddy. DADDY. See?" I gesture toward him with a wave of my hand. *Tada!* "It's the only way you actually listen to me!"

I slam my door shut and head toward the water. The wind teases my eyes, making them blink. *Cry,* they urge. *Go ahead. You can feel it, can't you? Cry-baby, cry...*

"Stop running away," Thorny snarls, his voice chasing me down the hill. He left the car as well, I realize, as his footsteps creep on mine. "Just tell me what you want to say. I'm listening. So talk."

He waits.

I'm silent.

He hisses. "You see? This is what I mean! You scream and throw tantrums to get attention, but once you have it?" He mimes grasping at the air. "Nothing. You bitch and moan about never being heard, but you never have anything to say, do you? Answer me!"

He's gaining ground, covering three of my footprints with one stride.

I change direction and practically skip toward the shore. *Whoosh!* The tail end of a wave laps at my sandals, licking up my calves and soaking through my jeans. When I look back, Thorny's standing several feet away.

"Let's make a pact," he declares. "You act like an adult. You call me by my name and speak reasonably, and I'll answer whatever you ask. Do that for me and I will never lie to you."

Oh? I plant my hands on my hips and purse my lips. "Why is Elaine fucking someone else? *James?*"

His eyes narrow, but in the direct path of the sun, he doesn't look as surly as he should. "Because she's a whore, Maryanne."

I swallow as shock makes me forget the millions of ways I could tease him. Taunt him. Make him redder and redder until he explodes.

"My turn," Thorny says, turning the tables. "Why did you have sex with a professor's son in the headmaster's office? Or why did you ruin Caroline's marriage? Why did you steal from Lily and destroy her family's SUV? Why does it seem like you go out of your way to make the lives of everyone around you all the more difficult?"

He sounds genuinely curious. But the answer is obvious.

I shrug. "Because I'm a whore, James."

Attention whore.

Needy whore.

WHORE.

My new favorite word. *Bingo!*

Now, he has an answer for everything. But it doesn't seem to satisfy him. He observes me, his jaw clenched, his eyes flashing and angry. *You never have anything to say,* he groused.

But what use are words? I've been screaming through my skin for so long. I'm more fluent in nonverbal cues than I am in English. My mother couldn't teach me French, but she taught me lies. She taught me how to smile sweetly while siphoning money from a wallet. How to kiss your victims on the cheek while rolling your eyes in the same motion.

Make lives difficult?

My mother taught me how to *destroy* them. At least I haven't followed that far in her footsteps.

Yet.

Thorny wants words. Frowning, I try to give him some.

"What happens if I decide I like 'Daddy' better than James?"

His arms go over his chest. "Then I'll act like your father."

My brain flashes to an unwanted comparison. Like my father. Charming, funny, and sweet—but unable to be trusted around neckties. Devoted to his only daughter—yet so in love with a woman he'd die for her, leaving everyone else behind.

No. I think up another reason. "You mean you'll spank me again?"

"I'll spank you again."

I freeze, suddenly aware of how tight my jeans are. The denim rubs my inner thighs as I draw my feet together. *I'll spank you again.* Only he could make it sound like a credible threat. His posture speaks volumes where he doesn't have to: his arms flex, his fingers twitch.

My bottom twinges. I can't deny that I'm tempted to say that little word once. Just to test him. But he's presented me with a harder temptation to resist.

"So, *James.*" I draw out his name, watching him stiffen from the corner of my eye. "If I can ask you anything… Then why did you take me back, really?"

It's a softball question I already know the answer to: *for the money, Maryanne.*

"Why?" he repeats so quietly that I barely hear him above the waves. "What else was I supposed to do?"

Oh boo. That's an easy one: he could have let me stay gone.

Made me a ward of the state.

Prove once and for all that it's *me*—I'm the bane of his existence. Even miles away, on opposite sides of the country, he can't ignore me.

I've won.

What else was he supposed to do?

Stay.

I turn my back on him and wrench my shoes off. Closing my eyes, I skip down the beach, darting in and out of the water's reach. It's so cold. It numbs my skin, paralyzing nerve and muscle—but the moment I leave it, my body longs for the cooling sensation. That deep, dark blue.

I wade a little deeper and it's even colder. More shocking.

Gasping, I dance onto the sand again, but it's too dry, chafing my raw skin.

Then it sinks in: I'll never get enough of the ocean. It will always be too vast. No matter how cautiously I approach, it's quick to shove me back with wave after wave. But a part of me loves resisting the push and pull. It craves the relentless cold, because…

If I can survive for a minute, maybe two, then it relents. I become warmer than I've ever felt. It's salty and prickly, but more soothing on my skin than the cleaner, harsher tap water at Thornfield. It's wild. I'll never be able to tell it to stop, no matter how hard I stamp my feet or scream.

It will always resist me.

I'll always try to stand tall against the onslaught.

I'll always lose.

horny walks back to the car alone, and I follow him, tainting the interior of the convertible with sea salt and sand. I shamelessly wiggle my toes while cradling my sandals on my lap. Then I watch the tan grains scatter over the plastic mat beneath my feet.

When we return home, we say nothing, retreating to opposite ends of the house like warring armies in the midst of a truce. Dinner for me is a cheese sandwich I fish out of the fridge.

For Thorny, it's a wine bottle with a side of two beers. He guzzles his meal ravenously, sulking at the ocean, his cell phone nearby. He's waiting for a call, I suspect.

But, as the night wears on, the phone never rings.

A knock on my door jars me awake. Painfully early, it seems. The sun isn't even shining.

"You have five minutes," Thorny warns from the hall. "Or I'm leaving without you."

Leaving? I lift my head, blinking back eye crust.

"Put on the uniform," he adds before descending the stairs.

It's a magic phrase that has me leaping from beneath the covers. I wash up and get dressed in record time, avoiding my reflection in the mirror. My bruises are purple, my cuts scabbed over and swollen. I look like a broken doll, crudely stitched back together.

Thorny is my puppetmaster, calmly pulling my strings from a distance as I dash down the steps. The moment I am in the car, he drives off. I watch him, squirming. He's wearing his starched professor uniform, his hair slicked back neatly.

If I didn't know him. *If…*

I'd marvel at how the sun plays with his features, enhancing them. His eyes glow a deep ocean blue like this. Especially when he's thinking so hard. It's sinful, that expression.

I try to be a good daughter and not ask questions.

Why?

Why?

WHY??

I play the maturity game instead and fidget with my skirt's hem. That stupid red journal is on my lap and I stare down at it, surprised I even brought it with me. Maybe to taunt him? I may be a terrible ward, but I'm a damn good student.

I've diligently followed his advice. Even the dumb bits.

Such as, *convey how you feel.* As if to spite me, that's the lesson he poses to the entire class when the last students trickle into his classroom.

"Writing isn't about a series of abstract sentences," he informs us untalented peons. I swear his gaze honed in on me with extra pizzazz as he said that. *Pay attention.* "It is about conveying, in words, the very things you can't express out loud. Those secrets you can't confess. The stories you feel no one listens to when you try to tell them."

He *is* looking at me, his gaze like a missile darting over the heads of his real students, who eagerly take notes on his every word.

"Writing is about making people listen to you without realizing it. Showing them what you need them to see. Sometimes, words aren't enough. You need something to draw inspiration from." He approaches his desk and fishes a leather-bound journal from a top drawer. "This is where I keep what inspires me," he tells us, opening the journal to the first page and holding it up for all to see.

We *oooh* and *aww*, aptly impressed. He's glued snapshots to the pages and written garbled notes in between. My fingers twitch against the desk. I'd give anything to have a better look. To peer over his notes and random thoughts with the same scrutiny he does mine.

I see a picture of a forest, Thorny. But, ah, I don't feel it. Describe it better. Write it better. Just be better.

Let me crawl inside your head and see what you see.

"Images," he tells us, "can tell a story at a glance that you could need a whole novel to describe. And while this isn't photography class…"

He reaches behind his desk again and withdraws another surprise: a cardboard box. He lifts the lid, letting the students in the front row get a peek. They squeal.

"Cameras!"

We all get one. They're shiny, plastic machines that dispense snapshots. Polaroids, Thorny calls them.

"I want you all to find your own inspiration," Thorny declares. "Find the stories lurking in plain sight. Try to put the impossible into words. Find a way to tell your secrets through layers of prose."

We're all dismissed with our respective missions. The rest of his little flock gets to skip merrily off to their next class, while I'm driven home. Jane is waiting on the porch steps, her arms laden with enough materials to beat basic English comprehension skills into a rock.

She sequesters me in the study for the rest of the day, droning on about all the many things society deems it necessary for me to learn before earning a magic piece of paper.

Thorny comes home late, when I've already retreated into my bedroom. He's on the balcony, I bet, drinking his dinner and waiting for Elaine to call.

She doesn't. At least, the lack of shouting makes me suspect as much.

Before climbing into bed, I finish my homework. My Polaroid camera offers a wealth of new storytelling opportunities. After all, Thorny said it himself: a picture is worth a thousand words. My scribbled paragraphs might not be convincing enough, but eyes are gullible and easy to fool. You stage two people in the right way, ruffle their hair a bit, and remove a few items of clothing. *Voila.* A platonic encounter can have naughtier implications.

They had sex. They only have to claim as much.

The eyes are the window to the soul, but the soul is an unreliable interpreter. It can see things all wrong. Find meaning in mystery.

It can make a girl wander from her bed at night and creep into a bedroom she has no business being in. It's empty though, like always. Its owner is too busy scowling at the moonlight.

He doesn't notice when I flick through the few items Elaine left behind on their dresser. A pearl necklace. A vial of perfume. A tube of pink lipstick.

I swipe it over my mouth and heft the camera while forcing a pout. Say cheese.

My nightgown is too revealing. I tug on the strap and make it loose. Before taking the shot, I smear the lipstick on the tip of my finger.

Flash.

Down below, Thorny doesn't budge. Not even when I sidle to the window and sneak a snapshot of him. I only captured part of his shoulders and his head because my hands shook so badly. *Oops.*

I start to tear it up. It's useless. There are no secrets revealed in the picture's depths. Just Thorny, always out of my reach, only capturable in bits and pieces. Somehow, I wind up carrying it, unmolested, back to my room instead.

The pictures of me, I tuck into my journal.

The one of Thorny…

It's not important enough to hide. So I shove it beneath my pillow, an afterthought. Like lint and dust and those forgotten things gathered in the corners. You've always touched them without realizing it—that doesn't mean they hold any sentimental value.

They're just there. Always.

He's here. Always. I grip his picture so hard that it curls into a half-moon shape. Not because it means *anything*.

I have nothing else to touch.

FIFTEEN

I don't mean to tempt him so early.

Breakfast is the most important meal of the day —the building block for the rest of the grueling twelvish hours until bedtime. A glass of orange juice and a nice piece of toast can make one's outlook A-okay.

Not red journals filled with secrets and lies.

Those could make a man choke on his morning glass of wine once he spots said sinful object, his eyes narrowed dangerously. Smiling wide, I prop my book against my plate and munch on scrambled eggs. I've got to give him credit, he attempted a real meal today, Thorny.

We even eat together at the table like a proper family. Minus the animosity. It adds flavor, like salt, coloring the way Thorny does everything he can to ignore me.

Until he can't.

He snatches my notebook when I'm only partially through my eggs. Upon flipping it open, he scours the latest entries. As he turns the page, my Polaroids land on the table like confetti. Surprise!

"What in the…" His face gets hard, his shoulders stiff. Cautiously, he lifts the one of my mouth, observing it with a calculated frown. Then he laughs, flicking it aside.

I blink. The real, deep chuckle was unexpected.

"Pathetic," he says, tossing the one of my shoulder. He grabs the shot of me in my nightgown last, observing whatever secrets may lurk inside. They make him scoff with disinterest. That one he throws so hard that it lands on the floor.

"I'm beginning to seriously doubt your skills of manipulation," he tells me, his final verdict. I'm not even worth the time he could have spent drinking his breakfast. He takes two deep sips to make up for it and pours himself more right from the bottle. "I mean, for fuck's sake, if you can't stage seductive photos, then what can you do properly?"

"You should know," I counter, my face hot. "*You* took them."

That's what my diary entry claims. Oh no. Thorny lured me into his room at night. He wanted souvenirs. My face may not be pretty anymore, but who cares?

He's a dirty, dirty old man.

"I'd never take those glamor shots," he sneers, insulted by the prospect. "Anyone with eyes could see that. If I were the lecherous uncle, sneaking into your bed, I'd want something real."

Real. I mull this mythical word over, trying to put an image to it. Real like Elaine, who needs a shovel to remove her makeup. Real like flowy, flimsy dresses with waist cinchers built in.

Real like a beach house overlooking a cliff, where the perfect married couple within doesn't even share a bedroom. Eventually, they can't even coexist in the same environment. They simmer through the phone lines, blaming everyone else for their fucking problems.

"James?"

He hunches his shoulders at my sweet tone.

"What does real love feel like?" I bat my eyelashes innocently.

He grits his teeth in warning. "What?"

"Love. I'm so broken and crazy I've never felt it for myself." I form a steeple with my fingers and perch my chin on top, giving him my undivided attention. "Describe it for me."

"Fine." He grates out a sigh, accepting the challenge. "It's when you care enough about someone that what you want doesn't matter anymore."

Hmmm. That definition doesn't resonate. L O V E. Sacrifice, he claims?

No. Love is inherently selfish. It's about wanting someone more than everything else. Nothing matters anymore. Just them. Their thoughts. Their opinion. Their affection.

Their hate.

You'll take it all; it's a zero-sum game.

"James, what is sex like? In your own words," I clarify, licking my lips. "I've had loads and loads and"—my

dramatic pause makes him take another gulp of wine—
"*looaaadddsssssss…*"

"It's hell," he says the moment I trail off. "It's dragging someone else down with you because you can't imagine anything else. It's base, wild instinct. Something more than letting a boy screw you over a principal's desk in a desperate bid for attention."

"It wasn't over the desk," I explain, eyeing my bitten, broken nails. "He was seated in Mr. Gammer's chair, you see."

I let him picture the scene. A stuffy school office. A horny young boy. A girl with no thoughts in her head other than the need to have all eyes on her always.

"I was on my knees. They found me with his penis in my mouth." Near my mouth, actually, but Thorny doesn't need to know that. "I had no clothes on," I add for dramatic effect. "The whole school was scandalized. And do you know what I felt?"

I lean forward, letting him flicker through the possible answers. I can see them dart across his gaze, gone in a flash. Did I feel satisfied? Proud? Slutty? Whorish?

"I felt…like I had a sore jaw," I say.

"Maryanne?"

Uh-oh. The ball is in his court now. He whams it over the figurative net. *Swish.* I'll have to dive in order to hit it back.

"Why do you take pride in pulling stunts like that?"

Pride. It must be something in my smile. The one that's making my mouth ache in the corners. The one I have to struggle to maintain, ensuring that it never goes slack, even for a second.

"Because it's genetics," I parrot. "Like Mommy, like Mary. Or Marie. Same difference. Tomato, tomahto."

"You think your mother did things solely for the attention?"

Oh. We're in therapy-land now. Thorny's steering this crazy train with no idea as to the cracks in the tracks lurking ahead. *Bang!* We crash-land into one.

"She left," I tell him, shrugging. "In broad daylight, like you said."

No calls. No postcard. She had another man, I think. Another family. Another life.

It's all details, details. The fact is: she's gone. Good riddance. Though Grandmama always did boast, "If I'm alive when Maryanne turns eighteen, I'll bet every penny I own that tramp will remember her daughter then."

"And you think you're like her?" Thorny phrases it as though it's a concept he's only just thought of. Give the man a medal; he's cracked the code years of therapy couldn't.

"*James.* Does it bother you that Elaine might be having sex with someone else? Getting all hell-sweaty." I gasp at the thought. "Soiling her own hypothetical principal's desks?"

"No," he says, his eyes narrowing further. "I never put it past her. I just never thought she'd do it with *him*."

Him. The man on the phone she spoke to with simpering eyes. The man in charge of her sudden "work"-related trip. It's not the fact that he lost her that makes him so upset during his many liquid meals. It's the fact that he lost her to someone else. Elaine's just a shiny token in a game, but now, she's beyond his reach.

Poor Thorny.

"Are you getting divorced?"

His eyebrows furrow as if he hadn't considered the possibility until now. Divorce. How unseemly. "What would be the point?"

I can't answer that. So I push my eggs around my plate with a fork and devise a change of subject. "James, if you were to take naughty pictures of me, what would they look like?"

"You shouldn't be asking questions like that," he warns. But he doesn't deny me outright. He merely waits long enough to make that boundary known. "I'd want something real," he says when a few more seconds have passed. "A side of you no one else has seen."

"Real?" I'm oddly curious. "Like my boobs?"

"No." He eyes me more intently than before, searching hard for an answer. His tongue taps his lower lip in warning.

He doesn't want to say it—I can tell.

"Your eyes…when you aren't pretending," he finally admits, his voice a dangerous rasp. "Your face when you aren't putting on a show. Your soul," he adds, flicking his gaze up to mine. "I'd capture that."

Those three words linger in the air, uttered in that deep, thoughtless cadence that betrays he's thinking. It's the tone that launched a thousand bestsellers, and it's directed at me. My words. My lies.

My *soul*.

I hug myself tight, electrified by the prospect. Souls are things people like me don't have. We're too damaged. Too guarded. We imitate empathy and compassion, but we can never feel them for ourselves. Love is a currency collected from others to prove how valuable you are.

It goes both ways, positive and negative. Turn the whole world against you and at least they care. Somehow. Someway.

They fucking *finally* see you.

"So." Upon clearing my throat, I change the subject a second time. "Is my writing getting better?" I reach across the table for my journal, but he grabs it first, holding it hostage.

"Better. But my character is still lacking something. A motive."

"Motive?" My tongue tingles as I parrot him. It tastes like such a dirty word.

"Yes. A reason for his behavior," Thorny explains. "Preferably what makes him stupid enough to prey on his young niece."

Ah. "But what if it's love?" I ask, pleased with my newly creative brain.

"Love?" His frown isn't as disapproving as it should be. Shrugging, he slides my book toward me and stands. "I'd love to see you try it."

A dare is a dare, and I take his seriously, seeking him out only when I'm ready to spar again. Words are my weapon of choice, slaved over for hours.

He's in his office. I find him gazing out of one of the bay windows, wearing that pensive expression that makes me ball my hands into fists. Piercing, blue eyes all stormy and narrowed, clenched lower jaw, and bottom lip skewered between two perfect rows of teeth.

I'm tempted to touch him the most when he's like this: brooding. So damn surly. A part of me itches to run my fingers through his hair and count the many ways he makes my body react: pulse hammering, palms sweating, heart swelling.

"What is it?" His eyes find me as I creep to the threshold of the room, my bare toes grazing the polished floor.

I lift my journal and watch his gaze sharpen with renewed interest. "I've finished."

His grunt beckons me forward, close enough to set my book on the desk and then scuttle beyond his reach. Hidden in the shadows, where the light of his desk lamp doesn't reach, I'm protected from his scrutiny.

Not that what he thinks matters.

It doesn't.

Not even as my breath sticks in my chest while he mulls the request over. I'm selfish, biting into his time, desperate for any bit I can chew off. It's only lately that he'll let me nibble. A minute there. A few seconds here. Writing is the one trick I've learned to get close to him, even if it's only through crumpled notebook pages.

"I'm busy," he says finally. It's the truth.

A laptop is open before him, and his fingers are studiously tapping the keys—the first hint of writing I've seen from him since arriving here. Gradually, the typing slows as he eyes my journal a second time. Sighing, he picks it up and flips it open.

The longer he scans the pages, the harder my teeth clench. It could be because he keeps it ice cold in here. To think better, I guess. The cold makes everything sharper. The view of the ocean seems more expansive than usual, a bloody sunset and stormy, gray clouds. Even the décor is enhanced by the atmosphere; the black leather of his chair gleams, as unreachable as the waves churning in the distance.

Finally, his eyes still over my final scrawled sentence.

"Maryanne…" He looks up, and I hate the way my stomach lurches. Like it's connected to a hook, yanked at the whim of his gaze. When he's surly and disinterested, the pressure loosens. But when those irises darken with an unreadable emotion, I'm jerked forward, on the tips of my toes. "I—" He swallows hard and looks from me to the pages and back again. Then he sets them aside.

I know better than to reach for the journal. I know better than to ask him out loud for his verdict.

The way he glares at his computer screen, says it all.

Some boundaries aren't meant to be tested.

They might break, and we aren't the type of family that fixes their problems.

We ignore them, inching backward out of rooms we aren't wanted in, leaving our words behind to stain the silence.

He's the only one who sees me, dear diary.

I'm the only one who sees him. Really sees. I know why he watches the ocean late at night. Elaine was wrong. He doesn't hate the beach.

He craves it. The water calls to him, and ignoring its lure is the only way he can still feel alive. If he gets too close, dips one toe inside…

He might never stop walking and he doesn't intend to swim. Drowning is sweet, tempting bliss.

He didn't leave me behind because of the responsibility. He lied:

*It's because **he** is **my** ocean. He always has been.*

He always knew.

And that terrifies him.

SIXTEEN

We survive another week without Elaine. Mainly out of spite.

Our only true interaction comes on the weekdays when he takes me to Walden for one teasing class. Then it's back to Thornfield, where Jane struggles to cram everything I need to learn into my brain by the year's end.

In the meantime, Thorny does everything short of jump off the balcony to stay out of my way and I continue with my homework.

A hypothetical Thorny, lusting over a hypothetical me, would want my soul…

Interesting. I pinch the tiny ridge of flesh sticking out over the waistband of my skirt and give it a wiggle. Is my soul hiding in here, lurking among the fat? It doesn't sparkle. Or glitter. Or any of the other dumb shit souls are supposed to do. It just exists.

I snap a picture of it anyway. Holding it up to the light, I don't find anything special or alluring someone might want remembered. I could just be a shit photographer.

But no. Thorny wants me to dig deep. He wants me to put myself in his theoretical shoes—as a pervert—and think using his theoretical motives.

Lust? No, that's too easy.

Curiosity. Yep. That's the dangerous one. You don't realize you're even feeling it until you're on your knees, peeking around a corner to watch someone mount the staircase for the first time in days, it seems like. Unsteady on his feet, he wanders down the hall, chased by a flickering shadow. I hold my breath as he passes my room without noticing that my door is slightly open, my face pressed against the crack.

He takes his time, coming just beyond the curve of the master bedroom. There, he hesitates, his shadow swaying behind him. He takes a step toward the doorway…only to turn and march back the way he came.

He's out on the balcony minutes later. I can hear him cursing under his breath while setting something made of glass on the railing. He lifts whatever it is and sets it down. Up. Down. Up.

Then he sighs so heavily that the sound resonates through the entire house.

Love is sacrifice, he claimed. And maybe it is. You can sacrifice your sanity and wellbeing using the whims of another person as an excuse. You aren't the broken one —*they* made you this way. They imparted the first lethal crack.

After that…

Who could blame you for falling apart?

No one.

I wake up feeling like Satan is kicking me in the stomach. The moment I sit up, wet warmth trickles down my legs. I halfheartedly peel the blankets back and switch the light on.

Did I pee myself?

I wish.

I find blood on my inner thighs instead. Mother Nature has made her presence known, as irregular as ever. I think she was due a week ago, maybe two. Long after I expected to be either institutionalized or in an environment dominated by other cursed females.

Thorny wasn't supposed to keep me this long.

I tear my suitcase apart, hunting for the rare stray tampon or pad I might have forgotten. All I find is lint and loose sequins.

Elaine, the good housewife, probably has a stash hidden far beyond her husband's reach. Sighing, I head down the hall and into the master suite, checking every cabinet in the bathroom.

So many secrets lurk beneath the Thornes' pristine marble countertops.

Elaine's on sleeping medication, with old bottles stacked in a pyramid on the left-hand side.

Maybe that's why Thorny stole mine? He thinks I took it from her.

I can laugh at that, even as I turn my attention to a bottle of shaving cream which hasn't been used in ages to combat the stubble growing on Thorny's chin—he looks like a fucking lumberjack now. He even has a fancy silver razor that prickles when I run my finger over it. There are piles of spare washrags and a neat array of beauty supplies.

But no pads.

Bashful, Elaine? I bet she went out of her way to hide such unseemly things from him.

Under the bed, then.

Crouched on all fours, I don't find so much as a stray piece of dust. This couple hides their secrets well, it seems.

I have no choice.

He's lurking on the balcony when I enter the living room. Surprise, surprise. There's no beer bottle in his hand though. He just glares at the sky, tearing his hands through his hair as if manually rummaging through his thoughts. *Where did it all go wrong?* he might be asking himself.

When did she dig too deep?

How did I let her hurt me?

Should I finally fucking do it? Sink or swim…

Elaine hasn't called in nearly seven days. She's busy fucking her mystery man and has forgotten all about old Thorny.

"I'm on my period," I tell him the moment I reach the mouth of the sliding glass doorway. He left it open and the whole house smells like the ocean. Like him: imbibed with salt and bitter, fresh things. "I need pads. Where does Elaine keep hers?"

He looks back, his gaze aimed toward my legs.

Most men react the same way when presented with the realities of biology. Men sport morning wood and women bleed from their "special places" every month. You'd think a sex that spent ninety-nine percent of their time trying to shove their way into said special place might be unconcerned by the occasional plumbing issue.

"Where does Elaine keep hers?" I repeat, resisting the urge to stamp my foot. *Daddy* is on the tip of my tongue. I swear it is. Until he looks up…

And he isn't frowning. "She had a hysterectomy," he says. "She doesn't have any."

I gasp and mouth that word to myself: hysterectomy. The tabooest surgery in all of female-kind. My teachers used to mention it in hushed whispers when referring to a colleague with ovarian cancer. Now, she could never have children. The horror!

Almost as horrifying as bleeding freely before a grown man with no way of stopping it.

"Fine, then." I stick my hand out. "Give me ten dollars and I'll walk to Thornton and go to the gas station."

"No," he says, rising to his full height. "I'll go get them. Pads?"

"Y-you'll get them?"

"Yes." He makes it sound so simple. So obvious. He'll drive to town in the middle of the night for feminine hygiene products.

Because...

"Why?"

He scoffs rather than dignifying the question with an answer. But I want one. I chase him into the entryway for it, hugging myself tighter as he throws the front door open.

"But—"

"I'll be back."

He slams the door. Not in anger, I realize as the walls shake in his wake. He left in a hurry for a reason I don't understand until now. It's this *house*, messing with his head, driving him to the very outskirts of it.

This errand gives him a way out.

But still.

Caroline's husband erupted in a rage when I dared to mention my monthly curse in his presence. It was sinful to speak of nature so crassly.

Almost as sinful as what he did to the babysitter when Caroline wasn't looking.

Blaming me gave her the easy way out. The way she could save face before their perfect neighborhood and perfect friends. Jeff wasn't fucking teenagers because he was just a perverted freak who lingered outside the bathroom door whenever I showered.

No. He was a wholesome family man whose life was ripped apart by a vicious, spiteful little girl who spit naughty accusations. How mean.

Jeff would be a great basis for my theoretical predatory Thorny. In theory. In reality, Jeff didn't love the ones he sought to corrupt. He didn't really lust after them, either.

It was power he craved. The thrill of being the one to pop his little conquest's cherry. The one to make her cry, "*Ow, ow, you're too big,*" like Becky did the day I caught them screwing in the master bedroom. A man like him thrived on feeling large and in charge.

It was the only way he could get off.

My theoretical Thorny is too damn stubborn to give in to such "base" impulses. No, he's after something more exotic. Something alluring enough that he'd try to find it in his irritating not-really-niece. Something dangerous.

He'd play with it, my imaginary Thorny. He'd want to be the only one who could ever say he claimed it: a hypothetical popped cherry.

But, while Becky just bled all over Caroline's Laura Ashley bedspread, my hypothetical Maryanne might experience far worse. She couldn't just wipe away the mess left behind and toss it into the washing machine before the lady of the house came home.

She'd be ripped apart forever. How dramatic.

Almost as dramatic as literally bleeding all over the floor without a popped cherry to show for it.

In the end, he finds me in the dry bathtub of the guest bathroom with towels all over the floor in a vain attempt to clean the mess up.

"I'm coming in," he declares at the same time I tell him to, "Leave the stuff near the door and go away."

Like always, Thorny makes a point to do the exact opposite of what I want. The door opens, revealing him standing there with a white plastic bag filled to the brim.

A box of pads. That's all he had to get.

He got me *two*, along with two boxes of tampons for bonus points. He sets them in a row on the counter. Then he tosses the rest of the bag into the tub.

I expect to find a receipt, but the bag is too heavy. One by one, I pull out the objects inside, feeling increasingly wary. A bag of chocolate. A bottle of Motrin. A heating pad.

My brain short-circuits as I eye the bounty spread on my lap. I should say something nice. *Thank you?*

My lips part and the wrong words spill out. "James. Did you *make* Elaine get the hysterectomy?"

He didn't want kids; he said it himself. But he didn't realize how women like Elaine operate.

We can be happy together, he probably told her. The answer is written on his face. *Get the surgery. I'm putting my foot down. We can't be together if you don't.*

So she did. But Thorny is a hard man to love. Affection from him is like wanting blood from a stone. He made her take away the one thing that could give her an unconditional source of love—that's why people have children in the first place. As a backup when the marriage cools and emotions wane like finicky waves.

Elaine couldn't stay in this big house alone, no siree. What else is a girl supposed to do but flock to the next source of pretty words and admiring looks? A woman like her won't remain beautiful forever.

And, now, Thorny's lost her for good.

"Good night," he says, storming into the hall. He goes the wrong way, however, avoiding the stairs and heading toward the back of the house. He makes it fully inside the bedroom, slamming the door behind him.

Oops. I said the wrong thing.

The mean thing.

The truth.

SEVENTEEN

*H*e makes me pay for that, old Thorny does. He leaves me alone with Jane for days and days. He doesn't even take me to class with him. I have to continue our assignment on my own, scribbling passages into my journal in between lessons.

He makes me feel strange things, dear diary. Naughty things in the dead of night when no one's watching. That's the scary part.

No one's watching. There's no one to scream for. No audience demanding I pretend.

Is this what feeling feels like?

The pages can't answer back. I raise my pen over the final line, ready to scratch out every single word and throw the paper to the wind. The moment I press the nib down, the floorboards rattle.

"We need to talk," Thorny demands through my closed door. "Now."

He leads the way to his chosen battlefield: the master bedroom. He waits for me to enter before shoving the sliding glass door open and stepping onto the balcony.

It's getting hotter. Summer is a sweltering bitch who likes to linger even after the sun goes down. A layer of sweat coats my skin already, and Thorny's hair is slightly damp with perspiration.

"What you said," he begins while curling his hands around the railing. "Did you hear her say something? Mention something?"

Oh. About children.

"No," I say, telling the truth.

"Really?" He scoffs. "Funny, because *she's* the one who didn't want children."

I wasn't supposed to hear that. It was grown-up talk, that mythical conversation which little girls aren't meant to partake in. It's like crack, they say. You get a taste and boom. You think you're entitled to something.

Like more brutal honesty. It's salt upon your bitter, fragile soul.

"You did?"

"Does it really matter?"

But it does. It does to me. I need him to say the right answer, the one I've consoled myself with all along: he didn't want me because he didn't want children in general. Not even ones attached to obscene amounts of money. That's why Grandmama tried to force him, kicking and screaming, to be a pseudo-father to me.

He all but spit on her proverbial—and then literal—grave.

For Elaine? My fingers curl, my nails digging into my palms. *No.* That's not it.

"I guess adoption wasn't an option," I croak.

He laughs. The bitter sound makes my stomach hurt. My period ended a few days ago, but maybe this is a lingering symptom of PMS?

"You always have to make everything about you, don't you?"

I frown. About me? Not always.

But him? Yes.

"Look at me." He grabs my chin, forcing me to face him. He's drunk. I can smell the alcohol on his breath, though his touch is surprisingly steady. And hard. He tightens it when I flinch, peering deep into my eyes, hunting for every little lie. "Do you want to know the truth? Really? Yes?"

Nervous energy consumes me as he tugs my head forward, forcing me to nod. "Okay then. *Elaine* is the one who didn't want you." He watches me to see how the confession lands.

Does it sting? I don't even know.

"She begged me to pawn you off on one of my sisters who, and I quote, 'already has that burden'," he adds. "Pleaded. I'm not the one who turned you away, so stop fucking treating me like it."

"Like what?" My voice is a whisper, empty and soft.

"Like…" He shoots me a look that robs the air from my chest. "Like I broke your fucking heart. Did you really mean what you wrote? *He is my ocean—*"

"Do you want to know something too, James?"

He becomes rigid at my tone, his hands clenching the railing so hard they squeak over the marble surface.

"Why she let you take me back now?" I add before he can cut me off. It all makes fucking sense now. Elaine is one sneaky bitch. "She wanted an excuse to leave, you see? But she was afraid to leave you *alone—*"

"Oh, is that right?" He looks at me again. Really looks. One ruthless sweep of his gaze covers my ratty, unwashed hair and my pink nightgown with the holes worn over the left leg. He hones in on the largest one, catching a glimpse of pale skin that quickly turns red. "What about you? Why wasn't she afraid to leave you here with me, if I'm so fucking unstable? Because we're so fucking alike?"

But that's where Elaine's true twisted logic comes into play. I remember the way she looked at me that first day. Wide-eyed. Relieved? "*You look so much like…*"

"I'm just a distraction," I tell him, watching how the water sparkles like glitter. "To keep you busy so that you won't wander down to the beach and do what she *knows* you've been dying to do for years."

God, his laugh *hurts*. It stings, mixing with the stifling air. "You think you're so fucking smart?"

"No," I admit, my throat tightening. "I don't."

He said it himself. We're too much alike. Angry, bitter creatures, desperate to lash out, even if we have to scream to be heard. We'll do it. Anything. We'll poke the bear just to make him attack.

Because violence is better than being ignored.

"I…" The hint of sea salt tickles the back of my throat and I swallow hard, spitting out the first words I can. "I wrote something new."

"Well, I don't want to fucking read it."

Fine. I recite it out loud. "He wants me to be honest, but I can't, dear diary. Honesty is poison. It's what drives everyone else away in the dead of the night—or the middle of the goddamn day. It makes them—"

"Enough." He grabs my arm so tight that I wince and grit my teeth against a gasp.

"It makes them hate us, dear diary. Because we can't pretend like they do. And that scares them. It makes them—"

"I said enough!" He pulls too hard and I trip face down onto the lounger. He's there above me, pressing his knee to the small of my back. "Stop." He means it. I hear the telltale hiss of a leather belt being unwound from belt loops and folded in half.

"It makes them run," I croak, grasping the sides of the cushion in anticipation of what I know is coming. I poke.

He reacts.

Thwack!

He hits me hard. Harder than I deserve. My body goes limp, and the next blow makes the lounger jump across the wooden flooring. *Bounce. Thwack. Bounce.*

"It makes them leave," I hear myself admit in between sharp, stinging strikes. "They leave us alone."

"You think I fucking want to live like this?" he demands, striking me again. "I don't fucking… I can't…"

He stops, panting into the night air. Beneath me, the cushions squeak with added weight. I'm being crushed. His face is in my hair, spilling warmth onto the back of my neck. Blood? It drips over my skin in the same way, sliding down beneath my shirt, inflamed by his breath.

"We're too fucking… We're too alike," he says, growling the words to the point of unrecognition. "Everything we do, we can't… We can never fucking please them."

Them. The wives, and the daddies, and the mothers. Those people always watching from the periphery, ready to judge.

"I'm sorry." His hand creeps beneath my skirt, sending every nerve on red alert.

I hiss between my teeth as his palm grazes sore, throbbing skin. He freezes and the pressure on my back lets up just enough that I could wiggle away.

But I don't.

My thighs part as I take my punishment, feeling moisture seep into the cushion beneath my cheek the longer he touches me. The contact stays over my panties, purely for him to gauge the damage he's done. He flexes each finger and then rubs. When I flinch, he stops.

"I… I don't know what the fuck is wrong with me."

He finally stands up and lets me go.

But I don't move.

If I close my eyes in this moment, I never have to leave it. I never have to face the aftermath. So I squeeze my eyelids together and count to ten. I did this once before, when my innocent, little eyes saw a naughty, terrible thing.

I reached number seven then before he came, drawing me into his arms and swearing everything would be okay.

This time, I don't make it past two. His hands slip beneath my stomach and lift. I'm spun around and pressed tight to his chest like a tiny, compact doll. He carries me into the house and down the hall to my room.

He lays me on my bed and closes the door when he leaves, letting me nurse my wounds in peace.

He lingers for hours after, in the hall. Pacing…pacing. Sometime before dawn, he gives up and heads downstairs, disappearing deeper inside the house.

EIGHTEEN

My eighteenth birthday comes with a bang. Literally. The car backfires and Thorny can't get it to start. Cursing and huffing, we face an ultimatum: walk or reschedule.

With money on the line, we can't afford to waste a second. So I skip upstairs to exchange my leather Mary Janes for a pair of sneakers. My jeans and my shirt should hold up during the hour-long trek, but fuck it. I take them off and fish my new dress from its pile of tissue paper.

Today is a day worth celebrating. I'm officially an adult and Thorny is free.

Hooray.

We celebrate in silence during the long walk to Thornton. Cars pass us, honking in nonverbal offers of assistance, but Thorny ignores them all.

He's especially brooding today. I let myself stare at him for once, eyeing every inch of my once almost-daddy. He's changed his clothes at least, but he still hasn't shaved. His hair is in the semblance of its neat, professional coif, but sweat makes loose strands stick to the back of his neck. He's dressed to the nines, my uncle. His suit jacket is gray, matching a set of pristine slacks far too fancy to belong on a body traipsing along the side of the road.

What a pair we make.

My new dress swishes and flounces when I walk. I'm like Elaine minus the elegance. I'm Elaine minus the angry husband.

I'm Elaine back before her grown-up mistakes. I bet she wore less makeup and smiled more. Really smiled in a charming way that made her eyes sparkle.

Eyes are the window to the soul.

Mr. Lawyer shields his eyes behind wire-rimmed spectacles once we arrive at his office, panting and sticky from the heat. "Happy birthday, Maryanne," he tells me. Those arbitrary words Thorny has yet to utter.

He ushers us into the back room and opens a crisp, shiny new file.

"It seems I…misplaced the last round of documents," he mutters. "Luckily, the originals are kept in a safe. Here we are."

Tada!

Grandmama's last will and testament is finally fulfilled. She got her wish: Thorny finally took me in.

And his life imploded.

Mr. Lawyer goes over the documents one by one, summing up what I already know.

One: Thorny's guardianship over me is terminated. Two, another specification courtesy of Grandmama: I won't be able to touch the money until after I graduate in—per Mr. Lawyer's calculations—at least three more months, given the amount of schoolwork I have to make up.

"You are willing to oversee her education until then?" Mr. Lawyer asks Thorny, who stiffly nods.

His face tells it all: He doesn't have a choice. Not if he wants his slice of the family money pie.

Then that's that. Thorny and I are dismissed with little fanfare and we begin the long trek back to Thornfield.

Turning eighteen doesn't feel any different than seventeen—go figure. I still have those naughty little urges to say things I shouldn't. Thorny is free. I'm nothing more than a boarder taking up space in his house until I get my diploma.

Therefore, he doesn't owe me anything. Not even the answer to a teensy little question.

"Elaine didn't want me." Or so he said. "Then why did you take me back? You wanted the money, huh, James? That's it, isn't it?"

His shoulders stiffen, and his sigh reaches me as we crest the hill. "Not now." He's tired. So tired that he stops short, his entire body tense with awareness. "Maryanne…"

His tone is a warning, telling me not to look as I draw up beside him. Not to stare at the unfamiliar black car in the driveway. Or at the beautiful, buxom blond strolling up the front porch.

She turns as if sensing us on the outskirts of the property. With one hand, she shields her brilliant, blue eyes while the other upturns in a graceful wave.

Even from this distance, I know she's not Elaine. She's taller, her hair blonder, her skin paler. Like mine. We even share a similar body shape, just like everyone says—something I wasn't sure of until I see her now.

Marie in the flesh.

"She's back," I hear myself croak. What has it been? Eleven years? Eleven long years without so much as a birthday card or a phone call. Coincidentally, eleven years when I didn't have a penny to my name.

Eleven damn years.

"Wait here." Thorny starts forward with his arm extended in a silent command: *stay.*

His posture is stiff and formal, but nothing fazes Marie. Her broad smile shines like a beacon as he approaches. God, it's like looking into a mirror. A blurry one, smeared with age, where everything reflected takes on a menacing edge.

No wonder Thorny is always so damn suspicious of me, if I really look like that.

Finally, close to the house, he jabs his finger at something, pointing. Then he must say something, because Marie's warm grin falters. She drifts across the porch as Thorny becomes more and more animated with his hand gestures.

I've never seen him so emphatic, and stone-like certainty forms a ball in the pit of my stomach.

He's venting. I can only assume he is recounting every naughty little game. Every time I got in the way of his peaceful life. I'm a burden, he conveys with a heavy sigh. Can she take me away? Please.

Her pinched face confirms as much as her eyes shift from him to the copse of trees where I'm holed up. She says something to Thorny that makes him shake his head as he turns and heads back toward me.

He's still so serious, frowning like hell. More than usual. He's…resigned.

"You…you should probably talk to her," he says once he's paces away. "If you want. She says she wants to see you."

"Why?" My voice is an ugly rasp. I've lost my spunk. My pizazz.

"Maryanne…" Thorny shrugs in that helpless yet authoritative way only adults can. "If you don't—"

"What's the point?" I sound so damn hollow. Defeated. As empty as the house my mother is standing beside. "I know what she wants. It's the only thing any of you want!"

Which certainly isn't me.

"Maryanne, wait!"

Thorny's shout ricochets off bulletproof eardrums. I'm running, racing. Through trees. Weeds. Fields. I don't stop until I'm knee-deep in frigid water and the roar of a crashing wave swallows the way I scream.

Some nightmares are far too silly to ever envision happening in real life.

Like Marie, my wayward mother, creeping back into my life on my eighteenth birthday. She went over ten years without sending so much as a card. But on this day in particular, she'd return looking like a model fresh off a runway, tainted with the sickly sweet scents of France.

I used to think it, but then I'd stop myself.

No one would be that cruel.

No one could be so selfish.

No one could think…

I'm that fucking dumb.

The ocean seems to think so. *You care*, it cackles, lapping at my calves. *You care. You care. It's why you're crying.*

It's why you're shaking.

It's why you're on your knees, choking on salt water, Maryanne.

You care. You care!

But I don't.

"Maryanne!"

Thorny's voice battles with the roar of the waves. He sounds worried. I know why. It could be jealousy. What if I do what he's been too afraid to?

Though, if I drown myself, how will he collect his check? I try to stand up, but the water is vicious. A wall of waves knocks me down, leaving me sputtering in the tempest.

I kick my legs helplessly, feeling my pretty dress cling to them. My lungs burn. My face is on fire. Desperately, my hands claw at the foamy surface of the water then across the sandy bottom. There is no traction. No salvation. I'm drowning.

Then air.

"It's okay. I've got you. You're okay."

I'm squirming in his arms, choking on gasps. He holds me too tight. We fit together like puzzle pieces, Thorny and I. I'm the right height to bury my face against his shoulder and smother whatever stupid, pathetic cries might break loose.

It's a sympathy ploy, of course.

And Thorny doesn't disappoint. "I've got you," he tells me, smoothing his hands along my back, only to hold tighter when I quake. "She's gone. I told her to leave. She's gone."

There's a hitch in his voice. He's too damn serious. Like he thinks he's helping. Like he thinks I need him.

I don't. Grinning from ear to ear, I pull back and meet his gaze through a screen of fat, fake tears. "I'm—"

Fine, I mean to say. *Hahaha. You fell for it. I'm fine!*

"Shhh." Thorny jerks me closer, smothering my screams against the front of his jacket. I can't stop fucking screaming. Shouting. And for once, no one tries to shut me up.

"I know. I know." He says each word into my ear so I can't ignore them. His scent is ingrained in my lungs, his touch forever etched into my skin. "I know, baby. I know. It's okay. I'm here."

But for how long?

A seven-year-old girl could suppress the memories of good, comforting Uncle Thorny, who smelled so nice, with the voice like thunder. Only he could make the bad thoughts go away.

Only he cared enough to tell me the truth as the world around me shattered.

Until he left.

"I'm here now," he says, guiding me back from the water and onto dry land. "I know you're hurting. It's okay. Just let it all out. You don't have to pretend with me. I'm here."

NINETEEN

Tearful birthday parties come to the most fitting conclusion on an upstairs balcony with a bottle of wine.

Thorny doesn't want to give in so easily.

But I beg and plead. It's my one present. The only thing he can give me in this moment to make me feel oh-so-special.

One little glass.

It tastes like ass. But I sip and sip while he sits stiffly on the lounger beside mine, eyeing the sunset.

"I didn't know what to get you," he tells me.

I shrug, unconcerned. After all, what do you get the heiress about to inherit everything? You get her liquid happiness in a bottle. Three sips in and I'm beginning to see why he likes the stuff.

It makes everything blurry. Less sharp. His frown has a fuzzy edge to it now. He seems soft enough to touch. So I reach out, letting my fingers graze his jaw as my stomach dances.

He frowns when I rub my fingertips into his stubble. "This isn't much, but…"

He's hiding a real present in his pocket, I realize. He pulls it out and I stare down in shock, my mouth open. It's a leather watch, like the one of his I stole. But this one works. Golden numbers are set within an ivory background, encased in delicate glass.

"I'm a real adult now," I tell him, awed as he fastens the golden clasp around my wrist.

An adult cursed with all the responsibility of growing up. No more reindeer games. Mature people are honest all the time. Even when it stings.

"Can I ask you something, James?" I risk another sip of wine for extra courage.

He nods and sets his empty glass aside, having already drained it.

"Do you think I have talent?"

That question haunting every teenager looms now, with the buzz of alcohol making it seem ten times more important than it did before. What do I want to be when I grow up?

I want to tell lies the right way. With pizazz and flair. Maybe I want him to read them. To constantly disapprove.

I want him to hear me in a way no one else can.

"Talent?" he echoes, treating the subject thoughtfully. "Yes, you do…"

But. I wait for him to tack on a caveat. My Thorny, he can never let me win a battle unscathed.

"But. You can't keep hiding from your emotions. It's not healthy."

"Hiding?" I hold my hands in front of my eyes and spread the fingers apart. *Peek-a-boo.*

He doesn't laugh. His tone alarmingly soft, he phrases a question that makes me squirm. "Are we really going to pretend that what happened earlier didn't?"

Marie? I nod and sip from my wine glass. "Yes."

"You don't want to know what she said?" His tone dips as though he doesn't really want to say. For some reason, he feels obligated to, I guess. What was that term? Honesty.

"I think I can guess," I whisper. Another sip of wine doesn't erase the nasty taste in my mouth. So I take another. Then one more.

"She said she wanted to see you," Thorny says, sounding so tired, so old. "I told her I'd give her every damn penny I stand to gain from your inheritance if she left right then, no questions asked."

I stop drinking as I register just what he said. No. I'm sure I imagined it, picking up on his knack for imagining fantastical stories. "I guess this means I lost the bet?"

I hold my breath, watching him. He doesn't scowl like I'm used to. Instead, he laughs, so beautiful and real. "Yeah. You lost the bet..."

"And?" I croak when he doesn't continue his tale.

His half-smile falls. "She left."

"Oh." Of course she did.

Marie being Marie isn't the fact that makes my heart feel too big or the blood rush to my brain. It's him. Every penny? Really?

I look at him, too terrified to decide whether I believe him or not. My eyes itch—it's this damn breeze. "I hope you gave her a receipt."

"Maryanne…" He shakes his head. "You can talk to me about things, you do realize? You don't always have to put on a brave face. I'm here. I'll listen."

I could take his words as a pretentious bit of lecturing—or the truth told from experience. Truth, I suspect, as he strokes his chin, gazing at the crashing waves.

So, maybe I could play just one little round?

"Fine." I inhale, puffing myself up with all the fake bravado I don't feel. "So tell me the truth. Why did you take me back?"

He frowns in that caught-off-guard way, his eyes narrowed and lips twisted. Finally he sighs. "Why? I think… I think I just got sick of the fucking silence."

There's so much lurking in that deadly, dangerous word. Silence. Like the kind lurking between him and Elaine. It's the theme song of this big, lonely house: endless, muffled quiet.

"You are anything but silent," he adds.

I flash a fake smile. "Thank you kindly—"

"But you need to learn how to trust people and let your emotions out sometimes."

The mere thought makes me giggle and I nearly fall off my lounger.

"Be careful!" He's there to catch me, sliding an arm around my shoulders.

Let my emotions out, he said.

"I feel strange," I admit.

Hot, uncomfortable skin. Creeping, crawling heat. Lungs that won't stay put until I inhale him, getting drunker with every taste. My brain is a ping-pong ball, bouncing from logic to that dangerous realm of impulse.

Logic tells me to let him go. Pull away. Uncle Thorny is frowning again—I'm holding him too close.

But impulse whispers a dangerous dare: *get closer*. As close as I can. Crawl inside his skin if I have to. Remember the feel of his heartbeat so that I'll never forget it. Spill all those dangerous secrets I never have to anyone else. Look into his eyes—really look.

They're so dark blue. I could easily drown in them, fade without a trace. Ocean? He's more than that: he is the fucking night sky.

"I love you," I say.

"I…" He looks surprised. Thoughtful. Finally, he thumps my chin with the tips of his knuckles. "I love you too."

And he means it.

"What's wrong?" He sounds truly concerned. He tilts my head back against the pad of his thumb, meeting my gaze again. "Are you okay?"

I'm not okay.

"I *love* you," I say, stressing the word like they do in movies. How my father used to scream it in my mother's face while she laughed. And laughed. "I *love* you, James. I love you."

He frowns, sighing. "And here I was, thinking we could have a serious conversation." He laughs and snatches my glass of wine. Still chuckling, he downs the purple liquid. Swish. Imbibed with the antidote to my poison, he can humor me more easily. "You don't even know what that kind of love is—"

"Don't I?" My voice rips from my throat, tired and broken. My fingers twitch, aching…needing. I lean forward, letting them curve around his forearm without permission. *Uh-oh.* I'm rewarded with the feel of muscle clenching against me. "It's wanting to drown—"

"Stop it." He wrenches out of my grip. "You try writing a few times and now you're a fucking poet."

"Listen to me!" I can't stop reaching for him, my fingers crawling over the rough fabric of the cushions. I inhale as they brush something soft. His shirt. Then I snatch it, clinging tight. Tighter.

He grunts, turning to physically brush me off. "Enough. Let go, Maryanne—" He grabs my wrist, shooting me a warning glance from piercing irises. They widen and narrow in quick succession. Caught off guard.

I must look different in the moonlight. Less evil, maybe? Honest? Real?

He grits his teeth without saying, his lips parted. "I'm going inside."

"Wait… Can I ask you for one thing for my birthday?" I'm being greedy. He's already given me so much. Time. Attention. A watch. But I'll always need more. Anything from him. *Everything* from him. "Just one more?"

He doesn't move, his eyes flashing and wary. They narrow further as I crawl onto my knees, coming to his eye level. "What?" he demands.

I'm too drunk to copy his wordy prose or put all of my lessons into action. He told me to express how I feel. Sometimes, it doesn't take a paragraph to do so.

"I just want…" My heart races as my gaze fixates on his lower lip. The damn muscle throbs, knowing the pain lurking at the other end of this impulsive request. Too bad. I accept the consequences. "I just want this."

He doesn't move when I shuffle forward, pressing my mouth to his.

He tastes like sea salt, and wine, and all those dangerous, delicious things his books whispered of. Kisses were like lightning, he described once. *Zap.* The main character was forever changed.

My heart gets electrocuted the moment his tongue meets mine. All those boundaries hardwired into me since childhood go out the window. I'm climbing onto his lap, inhaling him so deeply that it hurts. He's a piece of me that I didn't know was missing, shoving through my battered skin, making me whole.

But he's stingy with his bliss.

"Maryanne, stop—stop!" He shoves me back, wiping his mouth on the back of his hand. Anger like I've never seen makes him look like a giant fuming above me. "What the hell is wrong with you?"

Everything.

Eyes burning, I lurch to my feet, stumbling toward the doorway.

"Not so fast—" He snatches my arm, holding tight. His breaths fan my shoulders in harsh, dangerous succession. "What were you thinking, huh? What the hell were you thinking?"

Maybe about all those times we played our word games. How he rephrases my thoughts in ways I could only dream. The millions of times I've climbed inside his head through his novels but never managed to understand him one fucking iota more.

"I'm sorry," I croak. "I'm sorry. I'm sorry—"

"Just stop it!" He wrenches me around to face him, scouring my expression for the hint of a lie. His thumb grazes the curve of my jaw and he glowers as it comes away wet. "Damn it. I never fucking know," he admits, hissing the words into my skin. "I never fucking know when you're being serious or when you're—" He breaks off. "I don't know what you want from me. I can't… Just tell me what you want. I'll give it to you, I swear. Just tell me the goddamn truth."

The truth? It sticks in my throat as my vision blurs. I have to cough it up, mangling the phrasing. "I just… I just want you to love me—"

"For Christ's sake, can you be serious for five fucking minutes?"

But I am being serious. The hard truth I haven't wanted to face before now spills from me in three little words. I can't hold them back. "I need you."

"Need me?" He laughs, grabbing my chin in both hands. "For what? A juicy little tidbit you can add to spice up your draft? Once that's done, then what? Are you going to send your little notebook to Elaine? Maybe something more public to get me fired from Walden?"

I blink at him, sending fresh beads of moisture rolling down my cheeks. "No, I swear… I just need *you*."

Him. It's such a stupid wish.

His scoff says as much. "Fine. You win." Thorny and his mind games. He lets our lips brush—mine quaking, quivering ridges, his firm and unmoving.

I'm in shock, I think. Paralyzed.

"There," he declares, drawing back, his expression smug and punishing. "Put that in your fucking journal."

Put what in my journal? How he feels, maybe? I'd have to use dramatic words to describe it. Electric. Dangerous. Raw. *Terrifying*, to convey how he grunts in shock when I lean in again to slide my tongue along his lower lip without permission. God. One taste of the wine still lingering on his skin and I feel drunker than if I had drunk the bottle myself. My hands grab his shoulders and my hips wiggle up against his frame. Anything to get closer.

Feel more.

"Maryanne!" He jerks back and grips my waist to keep me at a distance. Regardless, my body hums, relishing the firm pressure of each finger. They're restraining me. Rejecting me.

It doesn't matter. Either way, he's still *touching* me.

"You need to stop making everything into a game," Thorny scolds. "There are some fucking lines you just don't cross!"

Like wanting too much from someone with nothing left to give.

"I'm sorry," I say. I mean it. I truly do, even as I reach for him. Grab at him. Claw at him, twisting my fingers in his shirt so he can't go. "I'm sorry. Please don't leave—I'm *sorry!*"

"No, you're not." His hands twitch to push me away only to wind up jerking me closer. Too close.

I can kiss him again, rising on tiptoe just to taste him. He can stand there rigidly, even as his lips part, just enough.

Just enough.

"You need me, huh?" he taunts against my mouth, sounding so, so angry. "Do you want to ruin my life that badly? Fine, then. Get me fired. Go ahead." A hiss escapes his lips when I don't pull away like he wants me to. Like he needs me to.

I stay.

And it's just a kiss at first. A kiss…

Slow. Electrifying. Deeper.

His hands creep into my hair, raking. My own hands are clinging to him for dear life. We're at the edge of a glaring red boundary—I can feel it, a sensation like balancing on the edge of a cliff. One wrong move, and *whoosh!*

He should push me away now. I tense, preparing for it. My heart thumps, steeling against the pain. I'm ready to fall alone.

But he keeps kissing me. Touching me. Drowning me.

And, with one swift motion, we both jump.

Our fingers snatch at my dress in unison. In seconds, we hike it up over my head and cast it aside on the floor. His pants are down around his ankles. I'm being shoved onto the back of the lounger while he climbs on top of me, grunting against my parted lips. Whispering.

For once, his words aren't frantic and polished. I barely register that it's his voice issuing the frantic murmurs of, "We can't. I *can't*... Fuck."

His hand brushes my shoulder and every nerve in my body sears on red alert. We're too close, breathing too heavily. He's touching me too high as my hands wander far too low, grazing his hips. Still, I don't let the fear set in until he slides my legs apart and drags my panties down, capturing the lace beneath his thumbs.

"W-wait..."

It's too late.

His hands grip the backs of my knees and I feel something start to push inside me. Hard. Splitting me open.

"Owwww!"

He stiffens at the sound of my scream, holding himself rigid while my inner muscles clench, resisting him. God, it hurts. It does.

But Becky was a little bitch when Jeff popped her cherry.

This pain...

It's sharper than anything I've ever felt. So raw that it chases away everything else but the need to keep feeling.

Everything.

Even his disgust. "You're a virgin," he grates against my neck, stiffening—trying to pull back. He sounds so damn confused. Horrified.

"P-please." I cling to him in every way I can, digging my nails into his skin until he goes still. "Please. Please. Please—"

"Damn it."

Fire. That's all I feel as he grunts and then lunges forward, sinking deep. Burning, tearing, searing fire that makes me jump and squeal and blink back tears.

But then I feel it: Him. Inside me. Moving.

He's slow at first, arching his hips as the sensation sinks in. His eyes widen with the terrifying realization of what's happening: all those red lines crossed. Inhaling deeply, he closes them tight and braces one hand against the top of the lounger, using it for balance to thrust again.

In.

Out.

In.

Whimpers claw from my throat. I'm shaking, clutching him with everything I have. Every. Thing. My lips find his and he pushes against me, nipping with his teeth as if in punishment for lying.

I'm a virgin.

And sex is hell, he told me. Base, mindless need. Twisting limbs and panting breaths. It's wanting someone inside you deeply. So, so deep. When your vision goes white and you can't tell where they end and you begin.

You know. You just *know*—nothing in the world will ever match the same level of violence. You'll never feel this good again. This fucking free.

This needed.

It doesn't matter if you're bleeding. Or if they're cursing under their breath, hating every second they remain inside you.

Because you both can taste the truth in sweat and salt and hungry, sloppy kisses: This is real. It's fucking real.

"Shit. I'm going to—" James breaks away, and suddenly, I'm empty. It hurts worse than being filled. I gasp and draw my knees together as he crawls backward and bucks into his fist.

One lash. Two. I feel the hot spurts of liquid on my inner thigh and my eyelids flutter. He's done that naughty, dirty thing boys do. Come. On me.

"Shit." He's on his feet, pacing back and forth. His pants trail from one ankle, dragging along the floor like a snake. "Shit. We shouldn't have…"

He looks down and frowns at what he sees. Me, my legs spread apart, my mouth still open. Shock is a terrifying thing. It creeps into your muscles and holds them hostage while you wait for the reality check that you know is coming.

This was a mistake.

We shouldn't have done it.

"Damn it." Thorny sighs as he bends and draws his pants back up, refastening them around his waist. He approaches me slowly. Hesitatingly.

I feel his fingers graze my shoulder before I hear his voice.

"Come here."

It must be the expression on my face that makes him talk like that: softly and gently. I'm in his arms again, but this time, he carries me into the master bedroom and then into that enormous, white bathroom with the walk-in shower big enough for two.

He has to hold me upright—I'm so damn tired. My legs are jelly, wobbling like a newborn fawn's. My arms are locked around his waist. He can't move without dragging me along with him. Water sprays down, flooding the narrow stall with steam and heat.

Eventually, he gets a washrag and soap. He works them both into a lather and drags them over my lower back. Then higher, up to my shoulders. A part of me doesn't want to let him go enough to allow him to finish. It might break the spell keeping him here. *Poof.* He'll run away.

It's stupid. He tells me as much, murmuring into my ear. "Come on. Let go. It's okay. I've got you."

His heavy tone of voice says it all: we did a bad, bad thing. He has to wipe the blood off to make it better and let the evidence float down the drain.

"Maryanne, let go."

There's a bench built into the wall of the shower. He steers me to it and hunches over to lower me onto it.

Almost immediately, he crouches and grabs my leg. I watch the rag dart over my skin, held by his fingers. The knuckles are white as he scrubs and scrubs.

Then he looks up.

I'm naked; he's not. His pants are probably ruined, soaked to the bone. With a trembling finger, he bats a strand of my hair from my face. Then he lowers his head and continues to clean. He makes a good go at it, old Thorny—but it's a bust. No matter how much soap he uses, I don't disappear.

He has no choice but to bundle me up in a towel and watch me drip all over the polished floor.

I'm such a good manipulator, according to him. So good that one look at my face makes him bite back the words I know he has poised on the tip of his tongue. The cliché ones Jeff muttered to all of his conquests once he'd gotten what he wanted.

We shouldn't have done that, Becky, baby. You're too young. I'm too old. I took advantage of your innocence.

He just sighs instead. "You're crying." He sounds horrified by the realization. Annoyed. "Just stop. Stop crying. Please." His hand grazes my cheek and he sighs again when the fingers come away wet. "I can't…"

He lumbers into the master suite and rummages around, returning a minute later wearing dry pants and carrying an oversized shirt. He tugs my towel off and dresses me in the shirt—his shirt. It even smells like him.

"Come on." He takes my hand and leads me from the bathroom.

I expect a quick and efficient trip to my room, where he'll tuck me into bed. This was all a bad dream.

He does guide me over to a bed, but it's the wrong one. The wrong size. It's big enough for him to climb on beside me and pin me down with the weight of one arm flung over my waist.

"Go to sleep," he commands in that surly, gruff tone. "We'll talk about this tomorrow. Just go to sleep."

TWENTY

I wake up knowing that the entire world is different. Things have changed like a reset chessboard. The old score has been erased and a new game is in play.

Maybe it's because I'm officially one year older.

Maybe it's because I finally lost that pesky virginity.

Maybe it's because I feel a sinner's breath on my cheek, quickening the moment he knows I'm awake.

"I need to ask you something," he says while my eyes are still closed.

I could doze off again if it weren't for the telltale warmth of sunlight on my skin. It's daytime. I crack one eye open and flinch; the room is flooded with yellow, more sun than we've had in days.

"I need to ask you something that could seem insulting," Thorny insists. "I don't care. I need to know."

Something heavy applies pressure to my shoulder, drawing me closer to a warm surface beneath my cheek—his arm, tightening involuntarily as if to keep me from running away.

"Did you… Did you plan this? Fake it?" he asks hoarsely. It's a question that kept him up all night. I can tell. My skills for devious manipulation must have no bounds in his mind. I'm *that* psychotic. "Did… Was this your plan? Get drunk. Let me—" He breaks off, and suddenly, his arm is gone. *He's* gone, and I slump against a wall of pillows alone.

Heavy footsteps tread the floor nearby. I open my eyes just enough to catch him pacing. He's still shirtless, wearing only wrinkled slacks. One of his hands massages his forehead.

"If that's what you wanted, then fine. You got me." He holds his hands up in surrender, laughing in a way that makes my stomach churn. Each chuckle rips from his chest, hysterically loud. "Just say it. Come clean. Was it all an act? Fake blood?" His gaze darts to my bare legs. Cursing, he changes direction to march away from me and back again. "Just tell me if—"

"No." The truth can seem so boring in retrospect. No wonder I love telling lies. They make everything sparkle like natural flavoring to otherwise dull conversations.

Why yes, Thorny: I faked my cherry so you could pop it with your big, bad manhood. I'm that devious. Hahaha.

"I didn't."

He slows to a stop. "I… I believe you." He doesn't sound like he does, so cautious and gruff. But he comes to sit on the side of the bed, his back to me, and sighs.

Poor Thorny. I've made him fluent in those heavy, exhausted sighs. They say so much without him having to utter a word.

We're fucked.

"So, you lied," he cautiously deduces. "About the other boys? And the kid in the headmaster's office?"

"Maybe…" I close my eyes again and release a sigh of my own. It's not fair, having to spill so many of my secrets. Honesty is cathartic, they say.

It's not.

He hasn't run yet. I have him riveted like those readers glued to his every word. *Writer*, I tell myself, filing the career choice away for later. There is so much power in wielding the truth.

"Sammy Kean is gay," I tell him, letting the cat out of the bag. "I wanted out of Whorton's and he wanted the headmaster to see his penis." Why? Who knows. Boys are strange creatures.

So are men.

"Son of a bitch." Thorny's shoulders slump. "I take it you weren't given much of a sexual education?"

"I know that the penis goes in the vagina and—"

"What about ensuring that your partner uses a *condom*?" he questions harshly. "I didn't. Do you understand the potential consequences? Do you?"

He means the scary words our female teachers used to warn about in hushed whispers. Pregnancy. Disease.

"I could have hurt you," he adds as though that's the worst part of this whole affair. More than the initial pain, he means. More than emotionally or in the figurative sense. He could have done physical damage. Sex is hell, after all. Sweaty, base, emotional hell where big, bad uncles get carried away while pistoning into their delicate, little nieces…

My thighs clamp tighter together, stirring up an ache I didn't feel until now. It's sharp and a little burning. Like something tore to make room for him. Popped cherry. A better word might be *ripped.*

"Aren't you supposed to threaten me now?" I wonder. He certainly has been dancing around the issue. "Warn me not to tell? Ruin your perfect marriage? Cost you your career?"

He laughs but not in that hollow way I'm used to. My ears sting. Was it real? "It's a little too late for that."

About the marriage part. He hunches over with his hands flattened against his knees and glares out the sliding glass windows at the magnificent view. His relationship with Elaine is a bit like those distant waves. There, you can still hear it. But you won't know for sure just what the status is until you toe the line between it and the brittle, dry land.

"Are you getting divorced?" I forget for a second that I'm not a true grown-up when he doesn't answer. I'm tempted to use his real name to see if that does the trick. *Tell me the truth.*

"I don't know," he says, shrugging. "It doesn't really matter. We… We need to talk about us."

Not him and Elaine, but me and him.

"Later," he clarifies as the totality of that scenario sinks in. "We need to talk about this later."

For now, his morning wine awaits. Sighing for the umpteenth time, he stands and staggers to the bedroom door, unsteady on his feet. Near the threshold, he pauses and looks back at me, still calculating, trying to suss out my real motivations. Am I a good witch or a bad witch?

Very bad, he must decide. So bad that I can't be left alone.

"I'll be downstairs," he says as if to warn me.

No jumping from balconies.

No swallowing pills.

No shenanigans, and most certainly, no nonsense.

I can't stand hearing the goddamn ocean. I wonder if it's the same for Thorny? Maybe that's why he and Elaine rarely sleep in here. It's like being trapped in a box with the real world yawning before you. There is an illusion of freedom and it is tempting to think you can escape, but if you step beyond these doors, you're not free. You are just in an outside cage.

I heed Thorny's unspoken rule though. I don't do anything rash. I creep into my little girl room and tug my clean, innocent clothing on. I brush my hair and grimace at myself in the mirror.

I do the same old things I've always done.

But, now, my old clothing feels too damn tight. I strip them off in favor of his larger, sinfully tainted shirt. Sensing that he's out on the balcony, I tiptoe down the stairs wearing only the light cotton.

Fresh air eludes me when I crack the front door open and stick my head out. It's just unbearably hot. I'm sweltering in my crusty, used skin—like a caterpillar stuck inside a cocoon with no way to stretch those shiny new wings I was promised. Being corrupted is a sweaty, stifling business.

Desperate for relief, I descend the steps and wander toward the only hint of a breeze. It blows off the ocean, carrying the scent of sea salt.

I follow the well-worn path weaving between the sand dunes and walk right up to the water's edge. It's shockingly cold, but the deeper I wade, the more I can breathe. Without a second thought, I leave Thorny's shirt crumpled on the beach and dive in naked.

Swimming was never my strong suit, but I learned ages ago how to float. How to lie back and let the current take you away while your own body does the hard work of keeping you suspended. I wade out beyond the waves until the water is as high as my neck and not as violent. Lying back, I let it carry me back and forth, gradually drifting down the shore.

The sun can't touch me in here. It beats down aimlessly, but the water resists its heat. Nothing can touch me.

But the shouting. It starts off faint. A distant murmur straining above the waves. Then louder. Louder, mixed with splashing. Frantic, desperate splashing.

"Maryanne? Where are you? Maryanne!"

My eyes jolt open and the spell is broken. *Poof!* I sink like a rock, sputtering seawater. My limbs flail as the current changes, displaced by a heavier body. Before I can brace my feet against the sandy bottom, strong hands cinch my waist, hauling me upright. I choke down fresh air as I'm steered unceremoniously toward the shore.

"What the hell?" Thorny's furious, his eyes blazing, his hair damp. He's still wearing his pants—as well as a fresh shirt he must have put on before racing out of the house. It's ruined too. *Oops.* "What the hell were you thinking?"

I laugh. I can't help it. He looks so serious, but I'm butt naked. It's a beautiful morning, but we had sex—so it's not. At least it shouldn't be.

It can't be.

Everything is different—his stern expression says so. Swimming in the ocean takes on a newer context now that

I'm a dirty, corrupted woman. I struggle, and he stops, furrowing his eyebrows.

Then he looks down and sees my naughty bits distorted by the water. Suddenly, I'm standing on my own and a foot of space separates us.

"I was just swimming," I say softly.

He's scared, I realize. His chest heaves up and down, his eyes wide. His fingers shake as he tears them through his hair, processing his overreaction. "I thought…"

I stop listening. His tone is too serious for today. My brain just wants to float and think of only trivial things. Hot sun and ocean breezes. Cool salt-tinged water and skinny-dipping. No adulting for today. No, thanks.

I can't help myself. My fingers dip into the water and fan out. Then I lift them and watch a stream of water splash him from forehead to waist.

He blinks. Licks his lips in shock, tasting seawater. His face goes redder by the second and I just know he's going to shout. Yell.

Instead, he turns, maneuvering through the water. Then he twists around. *Whoosh!* His muscular arm summons a wave that drenches me completely. I shriek, raking the hair from my face, sputtering on water.

"Hey!" I push at him with both hands. In retaliation, he grabs me by my waist and my stomach twists as my feet lose contact with the ocean floor. "No!" I claw at his hands in alarm, shrieking when something devious erases the previous concern in his gaze. "Don't! Don't you dare!"

He lets me go and I fall in slow motion. The water sparkles beneath me a split second before I land. *Splash!* I go under only to shoot up and throw myself at him, trying to knock him off-balance.

"Dick!"

We're loud, making noise that takes my ears a few seconds to recognize. Laughter? His is shameless and booming. Mine is cackling and high-pitched. I do my best to drown him, but he resists my every attempt until I have no choice but to latch onto him, locking my legs around his waist. I grab his shoulders for stability and try to drag him down with me.

But he's too strong and leans backward instead. I'm thrown against him, giggling so hard that I don't realize our foreheads are touching until his lips are on mine. My tongue is in his mouth.

And my nails are in his skin.

The first time was a fluke. I was drunk and so was he.

But this is too damn real. I'm aware of every hesitant motion of his mouth. How my lungs inhale his pained groan, and my nostrils flare, desperate to breathe him in. Consume.

Together, we don't float. He has to stand here, shouldering my weight as I slide my hands down his shoulders, peeling his shirt away. I'm clawing at the zipper of his pants next, but he shifts to let me tug them down, just enough to give me another biology lesson.

Erections. I've never seen one up close. Never felt a pulsing ridge of flesh against my palm before. Sammy Kean wasn't interested in me in the slightest. He didn't grunt when I snuck a peek at what lurked between his legs. He definitely didn't grab my hand when I hesitated, putting me right *there*, like he'd die if I didn't touch him.

I don't know what to do. I just let myself feel him, exploring every inch. Thorny shudders, grating out curses against my lips. In a good way? Bad way? I don't know. Our lectures didn't go so far at any of the schools I've been to.

I have to struggle to keep up with this new Thorny lesson. He starts to move, guiding us back toward shore. The moment my waist clears the water, he staggers forward and I land on my back, tasting sand.

Then him. He fits between my legs, better this way than he ever could on a shitty lounge chair. There's no resistance when he thrusts inside me. No need for leverage.

He shoves all the way in and I know I scream. My stomach drops like it would on a roller coaster. The thrill is too much. The anticipation is even harder to bear. Grunting, he fists his hands in the sand and just moves. Sinfully. Slowly. Violently.

I'm moaning. Gasping. Making all those pathetic sounds Lily did that one time I caught her and her husband having sex. "It's *sooooo* good," she told him.

But she was lying.

This.

Is.

So.

Good.

I can't catch my breath enough to tell him that. I can only bite at his skin and scrape at his shoulders with my nails. I feel like I'll explode if he doesn't go faster. But too fast…and I'll fall apart. In the end, he lets the waves set the motion and the water floods between us, washing our naughty deeds away.

I can feel it in trickles, licking heated flesh, heightening every grinding, electric bit of friction. We're dirty, dirty, *clean.* It's a false sense of security—we both get carried away.

Because I can't stop kissing him. Inhaling him. Drowning in him.

And he forgets.

One final thrust has him grunting in my ear. When he stiffens, my body tenses as naughty reality floods me in dangerous, warm spurts.

Lesson two is shorter than the first one. He rolls off me, panting, unconcerned as the sand sticks to his skin and gets in his hair.

"Damn it," he says to the sky. There isn't even anger in his voice. Just relentless, uncaring reality.

Damn it.

We don't have that all-important talk he promised on the way into town. He must have fixed the car sometime when I wasn't looking, because it runs enough to drive us to a drugstore in a town three hours away from Thornton. We get there just as the sun sets in the sky and ten minutes before the place closes.

Thorny goes in alone, leaving me in the car while Mozart blares to fill the quiet. He comes out carrying a paper bag, which he wordlessly sets on my lap. Then he heads back toward the southern edge of Frick, letting the classical music play.

A good niece would let him have his silence. He deserves it, after all, to contemplate just how badly he let himself fuck up. Perfect Thorny, he of the stellar judgment and golden wisdom. We screwed up *bad*.

"I'm not going to tell Elaine," I say.

There. That should erase his surly frown. Secrets are more fun anyway. Especially the dark, deep kind no one can ever know. I tuck him right there, beside my fear of clowns, safe and sound.

"Son of a bitch." He swerves to the side of the road and parks. His hands form fists that hammer the steering wheel. Once. Twice. Breathing deeply, he cocks his head, letting me glimpse an expression I've never seen on his face before. Brilliant, piercing eyes, knitted eyebrows, and a twitching mouth aching to shout something. Yell. In the end, he just grits his teeth and snarls, "Will you stop bringing up Elaine? She's not fucking here, and everything I do doesn't have to revolve around her."

But it does. Otherwise, that opens up our little predicament to new interpretation: not revenge. Something darker, maybe?

And that would be a dangerous topic for a young girl's mind to comprehend.

"You're angry with her," I say, like that explains everything. Angry people do things out of spite to hurt that nasty person in their life. It's how the cookie crumbles—in devious little crumbs.

Thorny laughs to himself, shaking his head. "You have no idea, do you?" He looks at me as if for the first time. A battered blond with too-big eyes, blinking at him from the passenger's seat of an expensive car. "You know what most men my age would say? You're a sexy, barely legal piece of ass and I took advantage—"

"Don't say that," I say, closing my eyes. Took advantage. *Eww.* Not what Jeff told his conquests. "I'm manipulative, Thorny. And I act too old for my age. And—"

"You're young." And he doesn't mean numbers wise. "You're so damn young."

"And it's too late," I finish for him. "We did it."

I stress *it,* that naughty word.

"We did." He scoffs. "Fuck. If people find out…it's not like it fucking matters."

His life is ruined anyway. Might as well go out with a bang. He scored a sexy, barely legal piece of ass. I pour over those words individually and then string them all together. Should they seem like an insult?

They don't.

"Look at me." He sounds too serious to disobey. So I lift my heavy eyelids and watch him, bathed in shadow and dusted with moonlight. "Listen to me. I took advantage of you—"

"Stop saying that."

"I did," he insists. "I bet you've never even had a boyfriend."

He waits for me to confirm that suspicion, but some cards should be held tight to the chest.

"I'm a big girl, Thorny," I say. "I can make my own mistakes. And don't worry. I'm not suddenly hopelessly obsessed with you *Single White Female*-style. You don't have to worry about me stuffing love letters in your mailbox or stalking you."

I wiggle my fingers suggestively.

He doesn't laugh. His eyes widen as if a sudden thought just occurred to him. "I've never cheated on my wife. Never. Not once."

I squirm, uncomfortable. "But she cheated on you."

We both frown as our confessions mingle, making the air too stuffy and hot. He rolls a window down and starts the car.

"I want us to be honest about this," he says, sounding serious. "To talk about this maturely. It happened. We don't have to pretend like it didn't."

But I'm so good at pretending—he should have been counting on that. He should be warning me not to talk. Bad things happen if mistakes come out into the open. Jeff had a whole treasure trove of text messages to Becky, warning her to stay silent, interspersed with romantic descriptions of her "bouncy little tits."

Thorny wants maturity.

"James?" I don't look to see how he reacts. I just watch the sky flicker by through the windows, speckled with stars. "Can I ask you something?"

He grunts in that wary, cautious way. "What?"

"What are blow jobs like?" I worked so hard to stage my scene with Sammy Kean, but even he didn't have an answer when I asked him. "For real?"

"Messy," Thorny says without missing a beat. "And you never give a guy one without a condom."

Oh. Good to know.

We say nothing else during the entire trip back, but when we reach the house, he gives me one of the items inside the paper bag.

Plan B says the colorful packaging. A simple pill capable of erasing mistakes. I swallow it down with ice water and curl beneath my rosy bedsheets.

He's pacing again, circling the entire length of the living room down below. He completes the trek once. Twice.

Then I hear him ascending the stairs and wandering down that long hallway that separates his room from mine. He crosses that threshold this time. The door closes behind him.

And the entire house falls silent.

TWENTY-ONE

*O*ur talk finally happens at midnight, when I creep into the bathroom and find him lurking in the hall the moment I attempt to return to my room. He stands there, bathed in the moonlight drifting in through a nearby window. One tilt of his chin beckons me closer, into that infamous bedroom.

A part of me wants to run away. My heartbeat plays a frantic soundtrack, urging me to escape. It's practically a constant, steady thrum. Instead, I follow him, inching forward in my nightgown. He retreats to a safe distance, watching me from the center of the room. Neutral territory, I realize. He even has an emergency exit ready: the door to the balcony is open, allowing the roar of the distant waves to pierce the silence.

"I want you to be honest with me," he says, his voice rasping. "Can you do that? Be honest?"

Uh-oh. That's a dangerous word.

Before I can respond, he adds, "You want something." A conclusion I suspect he came up with just now. He's a ball of nervous thoughts, Thorny. His hands rake at his jaw, grazing the thicker stubble. "Is that it? You want to go to Walden? Fine. You want Elaine upset? Fine. Just tell me what it is."

"Can I ask *you* something, James?" I'm eyeing the floor beneath his feet. It's stained with his shadow, distorted by every shift in his stance and twitch of moonlight. Deep inside me, I feel muscles tense with every flutter. "Was... Was it good? Was I... Was—"

"What?" He's frowning, wary.

Inhaling, I try again. "Was I too..." Terrible? I can't even say it. My nails pick at my wrists as my toes flex against the floor. "Is that why you think I was..."

Faking.

"Damn it." He's closer. Too close.

I'm enveloped in sturdy warmth as my cheeks catch fire and my words crawl down my throat.

"It was good," he murmurs low enough for only me to hear. The rest of the world is denied this secret. I'm the only audience of this particular tale. "Too good."

So good that I had to plan it.

Bank on it.

Cause it.

Use it.

Because otherwise...

What did it mean?

He doesn't tell me his own suspicions out loud. He holds me close instead, letting me breathe him in. Pretend. We're normal people the day after a normal first time. There's no hostility. No doubting.

Just grim acknowledgment of the consequences.

"I'm sorry I let you take advantage of me," I murmur into the cotton of his shirt.

He laughs in a way that sounds so, so real. Dare I believe it is? Maybe. I feel his grip jerk over my arms, loose and unsure. Then tighter and resigned a second later.

"*I'm* sorry," he says into my hair.

My lips curl into a frown. *Sorry.* If he keeps using that word so carelessly, I could get addicted to hearing it.

I might even expect him to say it the next time he hurts me.

We come up with new rules, heeding them in silent agreement without ever acknowledging them out loud. While in the house, we're the same. Surly Uncle Thorny and bratty Maryanne. I work on my schoolwork while he drinks himself into a stupor on the balcony.

Same old, same old.

It's only when I sneak beyond the boundaries of the old house that our dynamic changes. It's the summer heat, I think. It's so damn hot some days that you could lose your mind. The first time he did was along the path to the tree house. I'd been wandering the property after my lessons with Jane.

He followed me.

A simple walk through the woods became something frantic and grasping in the sun-dappled shadows. Gasping breaths. Smothered moans, swallowed by hungry kisses.

That's all we did. Kiss. Breaking away, Thorny adjusted his professor tie and backed away, nearly tripping over a stray tree root. "Eh… Get ready for dinner," he told me.

So I did, and we ate sandwiches and chips on the balcony in silence while the waves taunted us in the distance.

Hours later, I'm in my room, staring at the mess of dirty clothes strewn over the floor. Eventually, I gather them up and wander the rest of the house in search of a washing machine. I find one just off the kitchen, and I manage to turn it on—despite having never washed my own clothing in my life. Then I return to my room.

There, my weary sigh blows stray curls from my face. I guess I have no choice but to officially unpack. Though for how long? My graduation looms, a mysterious date roughly three months away. Luckily for Thorny and me, I don't have much to put away.

I place my two watches on the nightstand and drag my suitcase toward the bed. The only items remaining inside it are a cracked framed photo of Grandmama and seven paperbacks. I leave Grandmama in my suitcase, sparing her the chance to stare disapprovingly from the grave.

The books, however…

I carry them over to a white dresser near the window and arrange them upright despite their worn, dangling covers. *Wasteland* gives up the ghost and completely breaks in half, tossing papery dust into the air.

"Shit!"

Thorny has to have tape hidden somewhere. I take two steps toward the door before I notice him there, more pensive than usual. His conflicted gaze conveys damn near existential crisis levels of confusion. It isn't until I follow the line of his stare that I realize why: he's eyeing my private collection of the complete works of James Thorne. I don't think he's impressed.

"They're mine," I say in a rush. It's not technically a lie. They were Grandmama's—her prized, signed copies. But, when she died, I funneled them out of the house in my luggage and no one was ever the wiser.

"You've read them?" Thorny takes a step over the threshold without seeming to realize it. *Uh-oh.* He's toeing our fragile boundary. The walls of my room seem smaller, trying to squeeze him out. But he's James Thorne, crafter of magic words and conqueror of whatever he sets his mind to. "You've read all of them?"

He doesn't believe me.

"Try me." I place my hands on my hips, hoping the dare sounds more teasing than desperate.

"Fine." He points to a battered cover sporting a white house. *Murder Town*, his third novel. "How does it end?"

I roll my eyes. So easy. "The mayor was the murderer all along." *A subversion of the typical small-town trope*, one reviewer crowed. I never thought so. It was obvious from the start—the only man to smile, admired by all. Of course he had the skeletons hidden in his closet.

"And that one?" He's referring to *Swing*, my maybe-sort-of favorite of the bunch.

"It's open-ended," I admit, wringing my hands together. "You never name the killer outright. Most people assume it was the neighbor, but…I don't."

"Oh?" He crosses his arms and leans against my wall. It's as if he needs the support to face the prospect that I might actually have ideas in my brain that don't revolve around pissing him off. "Who, then?"

I tilt my head and eye the ceiling with a frown. It's ironic. He wants me to be honest—to trust. But no one has ever asked my opinions on things like thrilling crime novels or how they made me feel.

Go here, Maryanne.

Sit here, Maryanne.

Do this, Maryanne.

Listen, Maryanne!

"I think no one did it," I tell him, hating how soft my voice sounds. Hesitant, as though his opinion really matters. "I think it was an accident all along. A terrible mistake. Someone died, but everyone left behind needed someone to blame. Someone to hate."

"That's an interesting way of looking at it," Thorny says. He rubs his chin and eyes my collection with an unreadable expression. "Which one is your favorite?"

"Let me ask *you* something," I say, running my finger along the edge of the dresser, checking for dust. "'To the girl with the golden curls: I'm sorry.' It's the only time you've ever dedicated a book before. In *Swing*, I mean. So, why?"

He sighs in that heavy, ominous way. A warning, I think. But he's the one who wanted me to be open. Honest. Trust.

"What did you do to Elaine that was so bad you had to apologize in public?" I try to sound nonchalant. Like I don't really care what the answer might be. But my eyes never leave him once, tracking every nuance and shift in his posture.

"Elaine," he echoes, his expression stern.

"I bet you forgot her birthday?" I waggle my eyebrows and adjust my worn copy of *Whiplash*, taking care with the cover. "Your anniversary?"

"Did your grandmother know you were reading those? Those are first editions. I know for a fact that version of *Wasteland* is out of print—"

"I got them secondhand," I say with a shrug. "And I'm a big girl, Thorny. I can handle a murder mystery or two." Which brings up an interesting point. "What made you write them anyway?"

He frowns and shakes his head. "You can't just ask someone what made them write a certain story—"

"Why not?" I've always pictured him sitting at his desk, envisioning which plot would earn him his next cool million. His novels certainly shared a few running themes. Maybe he picked them off a list? Murder. Small town. Failing marriages. Death. "Is there some special formula to it?"

"Could you just write something if you weren't invested in the idea?" He raises an eyebrow and seeks the red journal on my nightstand. "Try it. I want you to try writing something without thinking about the person who might be reading it. Write for yourself. Something you want to say but can't."

Write for myself? I laugh even as I shift toward my journal and reluctantly grab it. Sighing, I flip to a clean page and jot down the first thing that comes to mind. Then I read it out loud to him. "I am not a writer."

Not like him. My words don't lurk in complex stories or brutal plotlines.

"Close your eyes," Thorny tells me. "Do it. Good. Now, tell me a memory. The first one that comes to mind. Tell it in a way that makes me feel like I'm there."

A memory. I try to resist mine, kicking my toes against the floor. "This is stupid."

"Tell me," he insists. "Make me see it. Make me listen."

"Fine. I'm in a room." Dark. Elegant. Decorated differently than his and Elaine's: sleek, with a view of the city instead of the ocean. But it's emptier in a way. The fancy furniture seems more mocking than comfortable. A constant reminder of who isn't there, draped across it, her hair spilling over the leather. "The world keeps spinning," I hear myself say. "But it's all…wrong. The sunlight hurts. The air in my lungs feels like glass. I can't breathe. And he's—"

"It's okay." Two heavy footsteps bring him closer. Too close. I can smell him from here, and my nose wrinkles, chasing his scent. "Keep going."

"He's holding me," I croak, my voice breaking. "And, for the first time, I feel something. I feel…"

The pain. The horror. The fear.

All of it.

"I want to scream. I want to cry. I…I want to die—but, with one touch, he makes it better. 'I know you're hurting,' he says. 'It's okay. But you're strong, too.'"

Strong enough to face reality. Strong enough to survive.

Strong enough for him to leave me behind.

"He made me feel safe. So safe," I whisper, digging my nails into the soft blankets beneath me. "He made me feel seen. Heard. Wanted. Alive."

Not in a creepy way. Just a *way*—I wasn't alone for once. He didn't try to shut me up or explain away the darkness I'd seen. *Your father had an accident, Maryanne.*

"He was honest with me. But then..." My eyes open, my story finished. I don't have to say the ending of the tale out loud.

We both know it by heart: *he threw me away.*

"You're right," I tell him, struggling to force the words off my tongue. "It's rude to ask someone about their stories. Good night."

I turn my back on him and fumble for my lamp. In the darkness, I burrow beneath my bedsheets, listening for the moment he leaves.

A few seconds later, he doesn't disappoint. His footsteps lumber toward the doorway, heavy and slow. Then they stop.

"He knew he hurt you," Thorny says, his voice loud in the quiet. "He'd be lying if he claimed not to. But you needed him, and he didn't know how to be that for you. What you needed. His own wife never needed him. His family didn't, either. The only time he felt of use to anyone was through his writing, but no one needed that, either..." He pauses, inhaling raggedly. My door creaks as if he grabbed it for balance, using it to stay upright. "He... He knows it's too late. The damage is already done. But maybe… You might still believe him if he told you he was sorry."

He leaves, moving down the hall to the room he shares with Elaine.

And I turn toward my pillow, squeezing my eyes shut.

It's the beginning of the weekend, and a day with no lessons is best spent wandering down to the beach, a towel in hand. I spread it out over a massive dune and lie there beneath the white-hot sun. On my way from the house, I found a package waiting for me on the front porch from one Jeremy Weston, of all people. As promised, he sent me a signed copy of his new book, along with his "stellar" debut from years ago.

I pick over the newer book first with low expectations. It's boring and pretentious, with a meandering plot that makes no sense and characters I want to bash to death with the spine of their own novel. It's exactly the kind of story I'd picture someone like Jeremy Weston writing: all blah blah blah with nothing real ever being said.

The second book, however…

It's different. The character has a voice that resonates, and each word pulls me in, painting a picture so haunting that my throat goes dry the more I read.

The plot is simple, in retrospect. A man is in love, but it's not what he thought it'd be. Less sparkles and roses and more like a shackle to someone else's wants, needs, and expectations. If he insists on his own desires, then he's selfish. If he says the wrong thing, then he's cruel. He feels trapped, like he can't even breathe without doing something wrong. Crossing the line.

And his wife is too jumpy to understand him. Too secretive. Her charming smiles hide a crippling sense of vanity, and he has to go out of his way to make her feel special. Wanted. Even if it means sacrificing everything *he* ever wanted in return.

It's a vicious cycle of give and take—until she goes too far and takes *everything*. She gets a hysterectomy. She pushes him away. But then, at the last moment, she tries to pull him back.

And it's too late. He'll stay because he can't leave—men don't abandon their wives. But something vital between them was ruined, shattered, and the novel ends with him convinced they'll never get it back.

"There you are." Heavy footsteps trek through the sand nearby, and I look up to find Thorny, painted red by a fiery sunset, trudging in my direction. "So, this is where you've been hiding."

He's been worried. His eyes keep darting toward the water and back. I wonder how long he stood on the balcony, scouring the beach for me from the house, waiting until the last possible second to come down here himself.

As if sensing my thoughts, he ventures too close and his bare foot tosses sand over my outstretched book. "Come and eat—"

"You wrote this." I'm not sure until I hold the book cover up for him to see and watch his expression change.

His cheeks redden as he gently tugs the book from my grip. He eyes it for so long that the sun has nearly finished its dip toward the horizon by the time he's done flipping through the pages. Then, without a word or even a sideways glance in my direction, he turns and lobs the entire novel toward the water.

"Hey! That was mine." I'm only partly horrified as the waves drag the book beneath them. "That was an autographed copy. I could have sold it, you know."

"Come and eat." He starts for the house, his shoulders hunched. "Your dinner's getting cold—"

"It was too good," I blurt out, watching as he stops in his tracks. "That's how I know Jeremy didn't write it. It's too real. Too raw. No one spins words like you do."

"Oh really?" He laughs. "Tell that to the critics."

"He stole it. Didn't he? Jeremy?" I remember Thorny snarling as much at Elaine during one of their phone calls. *That piece of shit stole my manuscript.* "Why didn't you ever publish it?"

"Because," he says coldly. "My *marriage* meant more." He gives the word a nasty twist that somehow says everything without him having to say anything else.

A writer may utilize his emotions for his art, but Thorny couldn't risk upsetting Elaine.

So he shelved his career for the sake of their marriage. The weight of that sacrifice has me bracing my hands against the sand for balance.

"Come and eat," Thorny commands. "Now—"

"How… How do I write like that?" I eye Jeremy's other novel. Apparently, words can be told wrong. Boring and lifeless. "How do I make something feel real?"

Real enough that the reader clutches their chest in horror as if the imminent peril is their own and not some fictional character's plight. Or words so real that the writer mourns them when they are stolen, I realize this, as he turns to face me.

He tries changing the subject. "Aren't you hungry?"

"Teach me," I insist. "I want to… I want to do that." I nod to the ocean.

"Oh, you do, do you? Then tell me what you're feeling right now," he demands, crossing his arms. "Don't think. Just say it."

"I'm feeling…impressed," I admit. "And jealous. And I feel like I know that character inside and out. Like everything he was going through, I was going through. I feel like I understand him."

"You're being honest." His eyebrows furrow as if he's startled by the prospect. Then he shrugs and raises his palms to the sky. "Well, there you have it. That's the secret. Ask yourself a question and be honest. Convey how it makes you feel. Confront the deepest, rawest parts of yourself and don't shy away from them. Dredge up all the fears that make you lash out or run scared and put them on display for the world to see. If you can do that, then you're ahead of the game."

"C-can I practice?" I don't look up from my wrinkled towel. Not until I sense him sit on the sand beside me and sigh heavily. I hold my breath as warm fingers sink into my hair —not affectionately. More like he needs an outlet for the nervous energy coming off him in waves. So he strokes. I roll onto my side, watching him, even as creepy crawling things escape from the sand and dart over my skin.

"Okay. Then practice," he relents, twisting my curls around his thumb. "Tell me something."

"Once upon a time, there was a girl named Maryanne. She was normal. She had an amazing father who loved too much and a mother who locked her in closets so she could go shopping—" I have to break off and swallow the memories. Then I keep going. "And she used to be pretty, but then her mean uncle Thorny pushed her off a balcony and scarred her face—"

He laughs. Really laughs, and I can't hide my expression. The one that makes him stop petting me and settle his hands awkwardly on his lap.

"But, deep down, she was afraid of being alone," I continue, my voice rasping. "Afraid of being left behind. And she couldn't say as much out loud because no one would understand…"

He says nothing, my lone audience of one.

He listens, even when my words stammer and make less sense.

Even when I cling to the hand he withdrew and refuse to let him go.

Even when the first tears fall.

He's *here*. Maybe that means something this time.

"All she wanted was to feel something," I say, concluding my sad tale. "Something without feeling *alone*."

Morning is a reset button, but I'm sure it's malfunctioned. The rising sun can't erase everything. Like what happens in the moonlight after stories are told in hushed whispers. When creeping hands peel off damp clothing and lines get crossed.

Again.

Thorny may shower for hours and hours afterward, but he can't get all the sand out of his hair. I can hear him upstairs, pacing away as I shove two sandwiches into another folded beach towel and make my way to the front door, desperate for fresh air.

"Wait." His voice chases me onto the front porch, where the sun beats down like a hammer.

For some reason, I can't look back, and it isn't until he slips past me and leads the march down the stairs that I realize he meant to wait for *him*. He's dressed casually for once, in a pair of shorts I bet he hasn't worn in years and a loose shirt.

I can't stop staring. When he's halfway down the front path, he looks back at me. An outstretched hand is my silent cue to follow and relinquish my beach towel. Together, we head toward the beach, casually avoiding the spot I claimed yesterday.

Despite the fickle sun, it's overcast. The clouds play peek-a-boo with the sunshine, making the water seem a brilliant turquoise and then a chilling gray within the span of a few minutes. Thorny leads the way, walking and walking until I recognize a jagged row of cliffs with a familiar structure perched on top.

The house looks different from down here. The lower balcony juts over a wall of rock, and from this angle, it's easy to see the decay lurking underneath: years of grime, and algae, and whatever else might grow on a beachside dwelling.

But then, seemingly in another universe down below, is a breathtaking scene of pure white sand, where the waves bleed into tide pools teeming with life. It's here, close to the cliff face, that Thorny unfurls my towel and sets it down.

"I haven't been down here in…" He trails off, observing the view he's so used to scowling at.

"It's nice." My awed sigh isn't faked. This place is beautiful.

I sink down, curling my toes in the sand, and watch the sun sparkle off the waves. After what feels like an eternity, Thorny finally sits down beside me.

Together, we stare out, saying nothing. But, in the same moment, we're saying *everything*. His hand is braced over the sand, close enough to touch if I want to. So I do, just to make him react. He draws it closer to his side, sitting more stiffly. Then he sighs. Sand and heavy fingertips dip into my hair a second later, coaxing me to lie on my side like a kitten at his mercy.

The best writing is drawn from inspiration, he said once. Inspiration found in the moments that contain too much to explain in one go. You have to choose the right words to convey them. Like *intoxicating* to describe a particular smell: sea salt with a hint of wine. Or *enigmatic* to describe a certain look cast your way by someone who thinks you aren't watching them. *Fleeting* to describe how it feels to know that this moment can never last. And *desperate*. That impulse urging you to extend the silence any way you can. It expresses itself in a racing, greedy heartbeat that gobbles at the blood meant for your brain, hoarding it.

I close my eyes as his fingers pick through my hair, and I dig my feet into the sand, anchoring myself to the warmth and the peaceful quiet. The more he strokes, the harder I dig and dig until my toes strike something hot and I bolt upright.

"What's wrong?" Thorny untangles his hand from my hair, his tone wary. "Are you okay?"

I swipe my hand along the sand near my feet, dislodging something small and shiny. Recognition makes my eyes go wide, and I laugh when I hold it up: a silver bracelet with a tiny seashell charm.

"Elaine does have taste," I admit. To survive so long without rusting, the bracelet has to be of damn good quality.

Thorny grabs it from me, observing it in the waning sunlight. "Taste, you say, but *Elaine* didn't buy this for you." He chuckles at the absurdity of the idea. "*I* did."

My mouth drops open—I don't miss the irony. Of all things, he picked a seashell. A token of the ocean I compared him to. Heart in my throat, I watch him twist the metal between his fingers, partly convinced he'll throw it into the ocean like his secret book.

"Here." He grabs my wrist, and I stare in shock as he clasps the bracelet around it. "Try not to lose it over any more cliffs."

"Deal." I draw my arm close to my chest, admiring how the charm sparkles in the sun.

"And there's something else I wanted to talk to you about." His real reason for coming out here, I suspect. "There's a program for creative writing at a college I went to upstate. Every year, they select a small group of new freshmen to qualify, but there's an audition process. It starts next week. Would you be interested?"

My mouth opens wordlessly. A part of me wants to lie. Nonchalantly quip *No, thanks. I'll pass.* But, in reality, I'm sweating bullets at the fucking idea of letting him know just how much I *do* want it. It's terrifying what the prospect of him caring about my education means to me. *Everything.*

"Can I ask you something first?"

He frowns but doesn't outright refuse.

So I take a risk and ask, "Why did you stop writing?"

His shocked grimace proves it wasn't by choice. Ten years without a novel. Ten years without putting his words down for others to understand.

No wonder he's been drinking so much.

"I—" He breaks off, eyeing the indigo sky. Suddenly, he leans back, lying beside me, flat on his back. His hands fan out, brushing my shoulder. By accident? Even as I shiver and let myself inch a hair's width closer, I can't tell. "Maybe I haven't been brave enough."

"Brave enough to publish?" I know that's not it before he shakes his head.

"To confront myself."

I inhale at the rawness in his voice; it's a rare glimpse of him without the confident mask I'm so used to him wearing. I wish it diminished him any. If anything, I feel like I did while reading his stolen novel: inside his head, nestled among his deepest thoughts, yet still so distant.

"Pathetic, huh?" he wonders.

"No." I shake my head, my words whispered. "Not at all."

"It's just... I don't think I'll like what I'll see."

But he's wrong. I have to bite my lip just to keep from saying as much out loud. The ocean is the most beautiful when it's riled by a tempest, churning in the midst of a storm. It's dangerous enough to swallow everything in its path.

And I think there's a mercy in that.

TWENTY-TWO

Our routine becomes so comfortable that it's almost *normal*, that icky word. During the week, I suffer through Jane's lessons while Thorny commutes from work to home and back. At night, we eat dinner in the dining room, talking about nothing in particular.

Later, we sit on the balcony and tell stories. His revolve around him: why he writes about murder so much, for instance.

"The thrill," he says. "A death can symbolize way more than just a death. It's an ending. A beginning. It's the culmination of secrets and lies. It's terrifying. It's all that makes us human bundled into one terrible event."

"Oh," I say, breathing the word into the wind. So poetic he is—even dying is more than the obvious: decaying in a dank, dirty hole in the ground. To change the subject, I do what I do best. Improvise impulsively without a thought as to the consequences. "Tell me something you've never told anyone."

He shrugs, thinking it over in that brooding, thoughtful way only he can. Finally, he sighs. "I've thought about divorcing Elaine once," he admits as my mouth falls open.

Coming from goody-two-shoes Thorny, the confession is the equivalent of a monk admitting he was secretly a prostitute. Deep down, a part of me squirms at the thrill of it, knowing something so deep. So raw.

But then I frown at the implications of what it means.

"Why didn't you?"

He looks at me sharply. The waning daylight enhances the panes of his face making him look older, but still handsome at the same damn time. "I bought a cabin down south," he admits, ignoring my question entirely. Kicking out his legs, he leans back into the lounge chair, observing the sky darken and morph in color. "I never told her about it, and I used to dream of just escaping down there with nothing but a fucking notebook and a pen."

He sounds so pensive, and I know better than to talk. This is his moment. His dream. Maybe it helps him to hear it spoken out loud, a confession good old Thorny rarely lets himself admit: *I wanted to leave.*

"I kept a spare set of keys in a safety deposit box," he adds. "It's been ten fucking years... Maybe I should finally sell it?"

He isn't looking but I shake my head anyway.

"Tell me something," he demands, turning the tables like always. "Something you've never told anyone else."

I tell him about all my lies. With flair and pizzazz so that he snorts and laughs that rare, real laugh of his. I tell him about why I hated living with Caroline, Lily, and Marcia—

because they weren't him. I tell him all about my many escapades.

It doesn't matter if he believes me or not. I think a part of him never will, not fully. All that does matter is that he listens. To every word, as the night wears on and the days tick by.

We're on the beach when I finally gather up the nerve to ask about that one pesky topic I haven't been brave enough to broach.

"Tell me about the day my dad died." I'm arms-deep in sand and seawater, making a sandcastle—attempting to, anyway.

Deep in thought already, he is sitting farther up on the bank, scribbling into a journal. "Maryanne…" His pen stills as he looks up, meeting my gaze.

I brace for his denial. *Not right now.*

"Please."

His teeth grate out a terse reply. "Are you sure you want to hear this?"

"R-really? I mean…" I swallow hard, nodding. "Yes."

"He called me that day," he says finally, setting his journal aside. "I knew he was struggling after your mother left, and I don't know why, but he called me… He loved you, you know. You *need* to know that. He loved you, but he had his demons, Maryanne. And I was too late. Believe me when I say that I'd give anything to have gotten there sooner."

"But you didn't," I croak, crafting sand turrets with trembling fingers. Such a shitty little castle. I smash it and start over from scratch. "So what happened next?"

"I found you," he says, his tone low. "You were so strong. *Too* strong. You just stood there—hell, you weren't even crying. And I knew that nothing I said could ever erase what you saw."

"My grandmother wanted you to take custody of me then," I point out. Grandmama was known for her brutal honesty. *Elaine couldn't raise a kitten,* she said of her own daughter once. *With Charles gone, Maryanne needs guidance, James. She needs you.* "But you said no."

"I couldn't," he says, shaking his head. "And not just because of Elaine, either. I...I didn't know how to be what you needed. You looked at me like I was some kind of god. Like I had all the answers, but I didn't. I *don't.* The sooner you realized that, the better. I thought I was helping if I kept my distance."

"But it didn't," I say, taking over the storytelling duties. "It made it worse. It made me feel—" I bite the words back. My sandcastle looms like a mocking, lopsided version of Thornfield—the only piece of it I'll ever truly own.

"Don't," he scolds sharply. "Tell me. Say what you need to say."

"You made me feel..." Everything spills out in a rush. "Like I was a broken, dirty thing no one could ever love. You threw me away. But I *needed* you—"

"But that's not true." His hand dips into my view, smoothing out the lines of my sand foundation as I blink frantically. "You never needed me. You still don't."

"Oh yeah?" I scoff.

"Yeah." His thumb swipes my chin, gritty with sand and damp with seawater, shutting me up. "And when you learn to face yourself, I know you'll be ten times more successful than I could ever be."

"But what if you're wrong?"

Because I do need him. I do. The words are on my tongue, but storytelling is about honesty. Knowing when to say the truth and when to lie. Right now, he wants to believe the lie. He has to.

"I made up my mind about college," I say instead.

He draws his hand away and leans back to observe me from a newer angle. "Oh? What's the verdict?"

"I..." My voice trails off as someone appears on the horizon, treading through the sand dunes, her blond hair tossed by the wind.

She spots us, shielding her eyes with the flat of her hand.

"Hey." Thorny trails his fingers across my cheek. "What is it?"

"Elaine's home," I hear myself whisper.

Home, looking tan and even more beautiful than before. She's swapped the flowing dresses for a pair of cream-colored slacks and a beige shirt with ruffled sleeves. They flutter in the wind as she stops short a few paces away, just staring.

Thorny doesn't move for so long that sweat paints my skin as the sun beats down, unbearably hot. Finally, he stands and faces Elaine. They watch each other warily, like wild creatures meeting again for the first time.

He takes his time approaching her, and she turns and heads to the house before he can catch up.

I watch them go, knowing that this is what he really means when he says to confront yourself. Walk toward that thing you've been avoiding, shoulders back, eyes forward. Allow it to lead you somewhere you might not want to go.

Never look back at what you leave behind.

It's the only way to feel the pain in all of its sticky, stinging glory. Like smashing grapes for writer's wine.

$\mathcal{E}$laine came home with her suitcase and nothing else. No divorce papers. No Jeremy Weston. It's like she never left for several months. In theory.

The reality is a stark, ugly picture. She's a crisp, neat puzzle piece trying to rejoin a framework that was damaged and warped a little while she was gone. Too clean to fit into the ugly gap left behind, she just sits awkwardly on top of the other ruined pieces.

She and Thorny talk for hours and hours, sitting stiffly on the balcony, their backs to the house. I watch them from their bedroom and follow their conversation without hearing a word.

She's sorry.

He's stressed.

She wants to work on their problems.

He's too tired.

She sighs at the horizon.

He drinks wine.

They play that game for hours, never really saying anything at all.

When he finally leaves, Elaine starts to cry, staring out at the ocean, while I retreat to my room like a good niece. Climbing onto my bed, I grab my notebook and scribble the million little snipes I'm used to saying out loud.

She's pathetic.

He's pathetic.

They're pathetic.

I'm jealous.

Oops. I start to cross that final line out only to stop halfway. *Lous* remains, the bitter half of a terrible word.

"You were telling me what your answer was."

I look up and find Thorny in my doorway, standing there awkwardly out of place. My hand lands over the page I'm on, obscuring the words.

He frowns but doesn't come closer. "So what is it? Yes or no?"

"Yes," I whisper, closing my journal and setting it aside.

It's almost ironic that the first day of the college admission test is tomorrow. Good. I don't have to sit there awkwardly as they avoid each other in the same room. I don't have to witness the aftermath.

I don't have to pretend like none of this matters.

"Fine," Thorny says, turning away. "I'll take you in the morning." He heads toward the master bedroom—avoiding

Elaine, I realize. She doesn't come up here, even as the hours tick toward midnight.

They're avoiding another fight, I guess.

And if I wanted…

I could make it one worth having. All I'd have to do is leave my little red journal out in the open for anyone to find. Like a morally compromised wife, perhaps? It'd be so fucking easy. So easy.

It's what I wanted when I wrote it in the first place. Chaos. I tell myself that even as I shove the journal underneath my mattress and out of sight.

Words have the power to destroy—Thorny taught me that. So does silence, when nothing is deemed important enough to say and the words shrivel up inside you with no one around to hear them. You just burn.

But at least you feel something.

TWENTY-FOUR

The next morning, I clamber into the convertible with Thorny as my surly driver. Four hours in theory should crawl by, but they don't. We reach the school with time to spare and no choice but to fill the empty quiet with something.

"You went to college here?" I ask as though I didn't already know that tidbit of info. Old Thorny probably fit right in among the ivy-covered stone buildings imbued with more age than even the campus at Walden. It's the kind of place I'd never imagine attending.

I'm the ditzy blond, always destined to be the party girl at some low-rent institution. Not here. My nostrils flare as if stealing away the scent of the crisp air, knowing I'll most likely never smell it again.

"There was my old dorm," Thorny points out, indicating a building across a sparse park. It's the first sentence he's spoken all morning, but his voice sounds level. Almost normal. "And over there"—he nods to a bench beside an old oak—"I used to write almost every day."

"About what?" I'm genuinely curious.

He shrugs. "About everything."

"Oh?" Everything from beautiful blonds to dark musings, I suspect. Back when he was brave enough to confront himself.

What might that James look like? For some reason, I can't imagine anyone more appealing than the roughened shell he is now. Weathered and beaten, just like Thornfield.

The rotten bits are part of their allure.

"Come on." He pushes the car door open and gestures for me to do the same. "I'll give you a tour."

As promised, he takes me through the heart of the campus, and it isn't long before he's spotted by someone who begs him to sign a coffee cup. Of course he's a celebrity here. The amazing James Thorne, spinner of words and twisted tales.

I sneak glances at him from the corner of my eye, watching how he reacts to the various accolades: barely at all. So stern. So surly. The attention doesn't even make him smile. If anything, his perpetual scowl deepens.

"What?" I ask, waggling my eyebrows as the last admirer skips away. "You don't like being recognized?"

"No." He exhales, turning his gaze up to the sky. A muscle in his throat jumps and I stare, wondering what confession he just swallowed down. "Not particularly."

"But it's nice, right? I mean, seeing how your writing affects other people. It means something?"

"When you put it that way…" He shrugs. "I guess so. Especially if that person is talented enough to write something ten times better than I ever could."

He looks me dead in the eye and my heart flutters helplessly as I fight to suck in air.

"I don't know. That's a bit much to live up to. You *are* the amazing James Thorne—"

"Look at me." He stops short and grabs my arm to spin me to face him. One of his hands flinches toward me only to curl into a fist and return to his side. "You've been quiet," he tells me. "Don't tell me you're nervous."

"Me? Nervous?" I try to smile wide, but he shakes his head.

"Stop." This time, he does touch me, stroking the corner of my mouth as if to wipe the fake expression away. "You don't have to pretend for me. You can do this," he insists firmly. "And…I'm proud of you for trying."

My face overheats. To hide the flushing, I turn my attention to a nearby building I assume to be a library. It resembles an ancient castle, plopped right here in the middle of a brooding artist's wet dream.

I'll never get into a place like this. Admitting that stings, and I'm blinking faster, swallowing hard. "Well, if nothing else, at least I can say that I attempted to get into the same college that produced the amazing James Thorne—"

"Stop putting me on a pedestal." He grips my chin in punishment, forcing me to face him again. "This isn't about me or what I've accomplished. I don't even want you to think of me tomorrow. This is about you. What is it *you* want?"

My lips twitch. For once, I don't want the truth to spill out. "I want to make you happy."

"Not good enough." His eyes narrow. "You'll fail."

"Of course. I always do—" I try to wriggle my chin from his grasp. He doesn't relent, and all I can do to escape is close my eyes like a child. *Lalala,* I can't hear him.

"Look…look at me, Maryanne." Sighing, he bats the curls from my face, and I can't deny his demand. "No more games. Tell me what it is you want. Not what you think you should want, but what you *really* want."

That's easy.

"You?"

He scoffs. Then sighs. "No."

His exasperated tone pulls a new answer from me before he can walk away.

"What if I want…to make people hear me. I want to make it impossible for them not to. I…I want to be an artist. Like you."

"An artist?" His eyes widen in a thoughtful way. He wasn't expecting that answer, I think. "Good," he says. "Then remind yourself of that. Every damn day if you have to. Never be afraid of the challenge."

"And what about you?" I can't help it. I'm nosy in his presence. I'm reckless. As I stand this close to him, it's like we're alone, even as countless other people pass us by. Breathing him in is comparable to drinking wine by the bottle—I'm drunk. "Are you going to confront yourself?"

He turns away and my heart stops beating for a second or two. I've never seen him like this, aged by a million years in the space of a second. His voice comes out a hollow rasp. "I'm going to try."

In what ways? Divorce? Confronting Jeremy Weston? Something even more disruptive?

He doesn't say, and I'm not brave enough to ask. I'll take his advice in baby steps.

"Maybe I'll look up Marie?" I'm only half-joking. Facing my mother feels like the epitome of confrontation. Damn him for making me feel—even for a second—like I could actually do it.

One day.

"Oh?" His face doesn't reveal a hint of what he really thinks. "You're looking ahead. Good."

"I bet you'll miss me," I counter. "After I graduate, I mean."

He won't, of course. He has Elaine and Thornfield. Namely, he has a life that doesn't revolve around me the way mine *always* has around him. Grinning wide, I cross my arms to shield against the rebuttal that I know is coming.

"Maybe." His fingers trace the curve of my jaw and I stiffen in shock. He's too close now. There's no mocking smile to counter the intimacy of this moment. Just stifling summer air and his body heat, making me sweat. Burn. "But maybe I shouldn't."

My stomach sinks, pooling at my feet. "W-why?"

"Because." He leans in close, grazing my forehead with his lips, and I'm paralyzed.

My pulse surges. My chest is a vice over fragile lungs and ribs. I can't breathe. I just close my eyes and feel him, memorizing this moment in a way unfit to jot down even in my red journal.

"I'll only ever hold you back," he murmurs, pulling away. "Come on." He heads for the car, allowing his voice to drift back to me. "Let's get you unpacked."

Thorny's suggestion is an unintentional turn of phrase: get me unpacked. But he already has. Racing heartbeat. Flushing skin. Dizzy little girl screaming to be heard. I'm a series of puzzle pieces assembled and reassembled by him— so many times that I've forgotten the original image.

His version is better anyway, a fragile thing, balanced on a web of lies. It's inevitable that she'll fall and smash into pieces—but at least he might help put them back together this time.

And even if he doesn't...his fingerprints are already on every shattered, jagged shard.

That could be enough.

We hopeful applicants are shoved into the corner of a dormant building, forced to stay in rooms we may not claim come fall. Mine is too small: a hole in the wall not meant for two people to squeeze into.

The halls smell like dust and old, forgotten memories—but this narrow space reeks of Thorny. Like I have the entire ocean lurking in my suitcase, along with a change of clothes and my brand-new watch. I unfold my pink blouse and my clean jeans, spreading them out over a lumpy, unfamiliar mattress.

"Well…I guess that's it," Thorny says after clearing his throat. He sounds too final, as though he's referring to more than just this moment. That's it: the end of everything.

And I don't want to hear it. *Lalala.* I curl my hands into fists just to keep from slamming them over my ears.

"I…" His fingers brush my shoulder in a hesitant goodbye. "I guess I should leave."

"Can I have a hug?" My heart clenches as his footsteps drift toward the doorway and slow near the threshold.

"I don't think that's a good idea."

"Just one." I'm whispering like it matters. Maybe if I don't speak too loudly, he'll keep pretending with me. One hug won't tip the scales between us. One hug and he can still go back to Elaine guilt-free.

It's just one hug.

I turn toward him when he doesn't move. He has a hand on the door, holding it open so that anyone who happens to walk by can serve as a witness. The way his gaze keeps darting toward the hallway gives him away; he wants someone to come.

But no one does by the time I reach him and encircle his waist from behind. He gets so stiff. I'm sure he'll push me off. It's okay if he does.

I'm already breathing him in deep to get my fix, sealing him away. Deep down, a part of me senses that it's for good. Writing was always his first love—and he threw it away to keep Elaine close. Their marriage is the balcony that stops him from jumping into the ocean.

We just won't say it out loud.

At least for these few tense seconds, he's mine, and I selfishly hoard each one. Inhaling, I press my cheek against the planes of his back, memorizing every curve. Every nuance and shudder as he sharply inhales and exhales with a groan.

"Stop…" He means it.

I feel him take a step toward the door and my arms tighten involuntarily. "Wait."

It's wrong. I know it is.

But he's the one who wanted me to be honest. Confront myself. And he was right: the real Maryanne is a selfish, foolish little psychopath.

I let my eyes shut, drunk on sea salt and wine. He smells even stranger outside of Thornfield. Sharp and pungent, but in a way that makes my mouth water, and my throat close up, and my stomach twist into knots.

"Can I ask you for one thing before you go?" I find myself blurting out, muffled by the fabric of his shirt. "Just one thing?"

"What?"

"I want you to lie to me," I whisper. "Just for a second—"

"Maryanne."

"I just need to hear it once. For a second, I promise." I'm holding him tighter. Too tight. A low sound slips from his chest, dangerous and unsettling. A part of me shivers in foreboding, but I can't let go. "Just once. You saying you love me."

"You know I love you," he snaps back. "Now, stop." He tries to shove me off.

I don't budge, clutching him tighter. "Like you mean it," I insist. "Like…"

Like how he talks about writing and playing with words and prose. Or the longing, fearful way he looks at the ocean, unable to verbalize what about it calls to him so much. I want him to lie to me sweetly. Sweet enough to counter the bitter, bitter end when he pushes me away again.

Because I know it's coming. With Elaine back, he has no choice. A man like him is a slave to himself, always at odds with his true nature. Now I know why he writes about death so much: it's the quickest, easiest means to an end.

Even if it hurts, someone gets their freedom.

"I'm not doing this with you." He wrenches away, leaving me stumbling for balance.

My hand catches the wall, and I watch him lumber over the threshold. Then he's gone. Angry footsteps carry him down the hall, echoing like the opening salvo of a thunderstorm.

This one will be epic, ripping me apart in the aftermath…

But it's still a ways off. Three slower, heavier footfalls bring him back, and he stands there awkwardly, dominating the narrow doorway.

"You don't know a damn thing about love," he declares, his voice rasping and hollow. "Describe it, then. What is it you love about me?" He twists the word, making it sound nasty.

I sigh, flexing my fingers as if I can capture his voice and unravel the tangled tone. I can straighten the twisted pieces out and make it whole again. The five-second rule applies in this case; his love is a little dirty but still safe to swallow.

"I love how you make me feel," I admit, surprised to feel the answer resonate in my stomach—it's *that* real. Love isn't how his books describe it as: cold, clinical relationships or functional marriages. It's stupid and simple, and it doesn't require a pretty sentence to convey it. Still, I try. "You make me feel crazy, and wild, and like…it's maybe okay to be those things."

My cheeks heat up as I watch him process that confession. He takes a step closer, shoving the door behind him. It closes. I jump.

He's closer.

"What else?"

My tongue flits out, wetting my bottom lip. "You make me feel…" Too much. I let my eyes drift shut and attempt to count the many ways. Ironically, I can only settle on one stupid word. "Good. Like I make sense. Finally, for once, I make sense."

Even when I don't.

"And?"

Alarm tingles down my spine as my face heats.

He's breathing me in with rapid, harsh breaths, igniting my skin. "What else?"

"You make me feel…weak. Like I'm a pathetic, broken thing who doesn't have to try so damn hard to pretend like I'm *not*."

It's terrifying to have my sarcasm stripped away and my lies exposed. At the same time, it's exhilarating to know he can see through me like a thin, wet sheet. I'm laid bare without trying.

And it feels so, so…

"Good," I blurt out, retreating to that stupid word again. "I feel *good* with you."

"And I thought your word choice was getting better," he scoffs in a disapproving tone, but I sense him grab my arm before I can flinch out of his reach. "If I loved you the way you want… You realize how wrong that would be, don't you?"

I nod. More than wrong. His love would be *taboo*, one of my vocabulary words: so many crossed lines.

"And if I did, it would be for stupid, selfish reasons. Like the fact that you listen." He laughs. "How pathetic is that? I'm a piece of shit who just needs someone to *listen*. And you're too… I'm not allowed to call you beautiful."

He's pulling me closer, holding me tighter. My heart churns out a frantic warning. A cue he must pick up on, because his breathing quickens as if in tune, following the same harsh rhythm. We're a symphony of destruction, composed more perfectly than Mozart could dream.

"And you'd know I'd hurt you, right?" he adds, his tone softer. Heavier. "Maybe I'd know it too, and I'd justify it like the ass I am. It would be the dumbest of excuses, too. Like the fact that you want to be an artist. Never tell someone that," he scolds. "What you want to be. It lets them think they might have a say in shaping that desire.

Don't you ever give someone control over something so important."

"Okay." My eyelids flutter, desperate to lift, but I can't. Not yet. Instead, I struggle to keep inhaling, committing this moment to memory. The smell. The taste. Everything.

"You *are* an artist," he insists, making that word sound so damn important. A subtle change in inflection and a stupid term can suddenly mean the whole damn world. "And nothing inspires like heartbreak. But I'd write it off, wouldn't I?" he adds as warm fingers creep over my hips, slipping beneath the hem of my shirt to scorch the flesh underneath. "I'd come up with some dumb excuse for why it doesn't matter, even if I *do* break your heart. I'd lie. But I'd know. We both would. I'd spend the rest of my life knowing that I took advantage. No—don't talk." His thumb lands over my lips, sealing them shut the moment they part, and I finally wrench my eyes open.

He looks so tired, Thorny. Eyes like fire. No, like the ocean, a deep endless blue. I have a choice of whether or not I'll drown. So I just stop swimming.

My lungs fill up and it's bliss. Intoxicating bliss that conjures more stupid, dangerous confessions.

"Maybe I want it?" I whisper.

"Of course you do." He laughs, sounding pained. "And *that's* what makes me the fucking monster."

The first kiss is slow. So, so slow. His lips match the trembling, hesitant pace of mine. It's an awkward dance of him bending down while I strain on tiptoe. It's nice in a way. And good. And all those other cliché fucking words.

But he's the one who encouraged me to broaden my vocabulary. The way he grabs me is sinful, grasping hands and sneaking fingers. They creep below my waistband, stealing the air from my lungs with every inch gained.

Sex is hell, he said once. But he was lying then.

It's drowning, being smothered by conflicting waves of logic and pleasure. The logic warns you to stop. You're gasping too loudly. Moaning too brokenly. People might hear, and the consequences…

Fuck the consequences. Pleasure is the antidote to reality's bitter pill. *More,* it urges. More panting. More touching. Feeling. Craving. Needing. More, more, more of everything.

It doesn't matter if you wind up on a dusty wooden floor with your jeans twisted around your ankles and someone's fingers sliding inside you. All you can do is arch backward, eyes on the ceiling, and whimper. You know it can't last.

That's the price you pay to feel alive.

And then you die.

Die.

Die.

Withdrawing his hand, he coaxes me onto my knees, brushing the curls from my face. His tongue is in my mouth, wrestling mine into submission as I claw at him with greedy, grabbing hands. Too low. I brush the cage of his zipper and he jerks back, grating a curse out.

"We can't," he says hoarsely.

Our gazes meet, wide and unfocused. Something in mine must make him stay and wrench my shirt over my head. Off. My bra follows and we're chest to chest, skin on skin.

Oops.

"Fuck it," he whispers when I tug at his waistband a second time. He bats my hands away and unfastens them himself, tugging the slacks down his legs.

Before I know it, he's on the bed, sitting with his feet braced on the floor. I'm between his legs, letting him guide my head lower, lower…

Blow jobs are messy. I remember him saying that. A sloppy, uncoordinated mixture of searing flesh and wet heat—but it's more than that. It's moaning. Rough fingers tugging at my hair and my heart pounding so loud that it's all I can hear.

Until he groans and my throat works to swallow, swallow, swallow.

"Fuck," he grates between gasping breaths. He falls back against the wall, his head tilted toward the ceiling, his lips bitten and red. His fingers remain in my hair, twisting and stroking my sweat-soaked curls. It's like he can't let me go. Not yet. Even when it hurts us both. His hands have to be cramping, and my scalp is on fire. "Holy fucking… Fuck."

I rest my head on his knee, closing my eyes as my body shudders, riding the frantic high of adrenaline. I'm crying, I realize. I'm laughing too, in broken, hysterical giggles. I'm coughing, feeling moisture running down my chin.

We're dirty again, but my tears wipe the mess away. There, all clean.

Filthy, shamelessly clean.

"I'd be sick if I loved you," Thorny says when our pulses slow and reality creeps back in, taking the form of muffled voices and laughter drifting from the hall. "Fucking *sick*. But at least…I'd fucking feel something. No one could blame me for that."

TWENTY-FIVE

There are fifty applicants in total. We're herded into tiny groups of ten, and on the morning of the test, each group is shoved into a room and given a writing prompt.

Mine is simple, almost insultingly so: *Write about your summer.*

The answer I come up with isn't so effortless. It takes me half the allotted time just to scribble one sentence. My seashell bracelet glints like a mocking reminder as I finally press my pen to the page.

This summer, I confronted myself.

And I hated her.

I studied her.

I learned what made her act the way she did.

It's not complex: she's a scared little girl in grown-up skin.

All she wants is to feel something: powerful, terrible. Anything.

But hunting for it doesn't mean she has to scream. She could listen...

To powerful words written in ink and stories no one else was meant to hear.

She can learn to speak in ways that actually mean something. To whisper loud enough to be impossible to ignore.

She can learn to trust...

And I think I could love her, that crazy bitch.

I think I could.

Even if her heart is already broken.

Thorny doesn't pick me up on the final day of the entrance exam. It feels off but not completely unexpected, if I'm honest with myself. He'll probably send Elaine to get me, with some half-assed lie.

Though who knows? Maybe this time, he won't even bother with the lie.

Regardless, I wait at his old writing spot while balancing a notebook on my knee. Pen in hand, I try to imagine what might capture the attention of James Thorne.

The heat?

The harried-looking professor sulking off to work in the summer?

Or maybe it's the expression on the hopeful faces of the other applicants. It certainly catches mine. They radiate fear mixed with anticipation. Who knows what they wrote about or what might separate the winning ten essays from the rest.

They say art is subjective; I guess that's true. Some tiny nuances in day-to-day life might go unnoticed by some and yet be impossible to be ignored by others.

Like the pair of officers dressed in uniform who make their way across the park. They're hunting for someone, muttering amongst themselves. Upon spotting me, one of them looks down at a slip of paper in his hand and then back again. I bristle uncomfortably as he comes closer.

"Are you Maryanne Mayweather?" he asks.

When I nod, the other one approaches me as well. Together, they stand there, their expressions like matching blank stares worn by action figures. Their presence isn't a soothing one. I don't think it's meant to be. It is clear they serve just one purpose in life: to deliver bad news in monotone voices.

"I'm afraid you'll have to come with us," they tell me in somber tones. The rest of what they say I catch only in snippets. Pieces of information my brain struggles to string together as my notebook slips from my grasp and lands open at my feet.

Only one phrase actually registers in the end.

Thorny won't be coming for me any time soon.

His wife is dead.

TWENTY-SIX

Thornfield Manor is a hive of activity, the likes of which it only seems to experience after a sudden death. Thorny's sisters are waiting when I arrive, all three of them. They eye me like something found stuck to the bottom of a shoe but do their best to smile through their tears and hug me anyway.

Because hugs make everything better. Even if we aren't allowed to go inside the house or speak to the prime suspect.

"They're questioning him," Caroline says, referring to her brother. "But I don't know why. It was an accident. A terrible *accident*."

She clings to that word, desperate to believe it. They all are, and they take turns uttering that magic word as the police shift through the house, feeding us bits of information at a time.

The preliminary consensus is Elaine's death was swift and sudden. Somehow, someway, she fell off the upstairs balcony, breaking her neck, but they found no signs of foul play.

Still, they have to follow protocol. Which means Thorny was ushered into the back of a police car and taken in for "questioning." Already, news vans are circling the outskirts of the property, desperate for a hint of red meat to feed on.

If only they knew.

My little red journal is missing. I know that even before we're finally led inside and allowed to access a narrow sliver of the house so that I can gather my belongings. A silent police officer is my lone escort who follows me through the deserted entryway and up the winding staircase as my stomach drops with every step.

Yellow caution tape and a horde of police cordon off the rest of the hall. Elaine fell from the master bedroom, it seems. From experience, I know that the investigators will pore over every flaw in the railing and every bit of dust. They'll sift through the untouched toiletries in the bathroom and the abandoned master bed.

My room looks just how I left it, at least. But, when I risk sliding my hand beneath the mattress, I find nothing. Just the edges of my old legal file and nothing else.

She found it. Elaine wanted to do a little spring cleaning to feel useful again. She may not be a faithful wife, but she can clean like one—*could*. My heart lurches at the use of past tense.

She *could* clean with the best of them all.

But then she found a naughty diary filled with sordid, lurid stories about her perfect husband. She wouldn't know that they were only that—stories. She'd race to confront him, shoving the journal in his face. *How could you?*

And Thorny, always the stoic, would ignore her. Though, no matter how many times I spin that scenario around in my brain, I can't envision the scenario where he would push her off. Ever.

Thorny was Thorny. He didn't feel anything outside of a crippling sense of despair that led him to drinking. And, even drunk, he'd be too apathetic to resort to violence.

Right?

I chant the answer to myself over and over, leaving no room for anything else. *Yesyesyesyesyesyesyes.*

"Are you all right?" The police officer sounds annoyed.

"W-what?" I flinch, realizing that my face is wet. I'm breathing too loudly, choking on the hot air. My fingers try desperately to swipe the moisture away, but it's no use.

It's funny. An army of psychiatric professionals spent years trying to make me acknowledge guilt. *Remorse is important,* they said. *It can serve as a block against impulsive behavior. You need to learn to take responsibility for your actions, Maryanne.*

But they were wrong.

Guilt is pain. So sharp that you close your eyes against it and curl into a ball on the floor, hugging your knees to your chest. You'd take it all back—every bad, bad thing.

You'd give anything—everything you had—to take it back.

They release Thorny shortly after four a.m., but he's not allowed to return to Thornfield. Marcia's husband has to drive an hour away into the next town over to pick him up from the sheriff's office.

I wait for them on the front porch of the tiny two-story rancher they rented for the night. It's old and reeks of rotting wood and dust. When car headlights illuminate the driveway, I lurch to my feet, hugging my arms to my chest. Marcia's husband exits the tiny rental car first, but after a second of waiting, I realize the passenger's side is empty.

Apparently, Thorny wanted to stay at a motel on his own. Away from us.

Or away from *me*.

TWENTY-SEVEN

The official story is that Elaine's death was an accident, like Caroline insisted. A terrible, terrible accident.

But, as far as the media is concerned, there's enough gray there to shade in with hues of intrigue. Oh no, Thorny, the reclusive has-been, had a blood alcohol level well above the legal limit when he was taken in for questioning.

Elaine was so, so pretty.

He was so, so angry.

The logical conclusion was that he killed her, of course. Murderers can't teach little girls, so he resigned from Walden barely a day after being cleared. By the end of the week, he was back at Thornfield, trudging through the empty halls.

Without the money from my inheritance, he might be forced to sell the property. So much for Grandmama's wishes—though even she couldn't have predicted the twist in her favorite son-in-law's perfect life.

I don't graduate until the end of the month—in fourteen days. Technically, I'm still under his custody, but Caroline, Marcia, and Lily argue the entire trip back to Frick Island about the risks of sending me back.

He doesn't need the stress.

He doesn't need the bother.

Someone else should take me in, just until I can claim my inheritance.

But not one of them has volunteered by the time we pull into Thornfield's winding driveway.

Thorny isn't waiting for me on the front steps. I don't find him in the entryway, either, when I escape from the car and race inside. He's not in the ramshackle living room or the disheveled upstairs hallway.

He isn't even on the balcony, glowering in his favorite spot. I finally find him in his office, slumped over the desk, a glass in hand. I sniff the air, eyeing the suspicious liquid inside. It's clear. Odorless.

Water.

"You're back." He sounds surprised as he lifts his head, eyeing me through a bloodshot gaze. A frown has become a permanent fixture on his face now, distorting his mouth into a stern line. "Why? Caroline or Marcia should have—"

"It's just for two weeks," I croak, wringing my fingers together. Like I have the right to plead for that much. It's only two weeks of his life. The life I destroyed.

He's hard at work, I realize as he sits straighter and shuffles a stack of documents on the desk. A story? Or legal papers dealing with the fallout of Elaine's death?

I can't tell, and I don't ask.

I've imagined this moment so many times during the seventy-two hours he's been gone. I'd smirk and utter something funny. Something quippy. He'd snipe back like old times.

Then he'd say it. Those terrible words keeping me up at night: *this is your fault.*

As I stand here now, nothing is the way I imagined it. Not even close. The words I dreaded hearing him utter come spilling out of my own mouth as I hastily rewrite my own script. "This is my fault." Heat sears my eyes and they well over. Moisture falls unchallenged down my cheeks and I don't even try to wipe the drops away. "I'm so sorry. I'm sorry—"

"Why?" He spits the word out, frowning as if he truly doesn't get it.

Why?

"Because…" I tug at my hair, hating him for making me say it. "She read my journal."

He laughs and my heart sinks. It's the most beautiful, broken sound I've ever heard.

"Your journal," he echoes as he wrestles his papers into a neat stack and sets them aside. "Of course you think this has something do to with you." He frowns and then shrugs. "Though I guess maybe it does."

Something catches his eye; instinctively, my gaze follows his to the book lying askew on a nearby shelf.

"I need to ask you something, Maryanne. The dedication in *Swing*. To the girl with the golden curls. What made you think it was for Elaine?"

I blink, confused. "W-what?"

"It wasn't," he says simply, meeting my gaze. "It wasn't about her. It was never about her." He stands and pushes past me, heading for the door. "And don't blame yourself. What happened had nothing to do with you—"

"Nothing to do with me? It had everything to do with me. It was my journal. My words." I'm shouting, and his sisters call from the front of the house, alarmed. They'll rush back here, viewing the damage. But, for once, I don't care who sees. I'm crying. I'm broken.

And Thorny is calmer than I've seen him in years. Not since…

Well, since the day we found my father.

"This is all my fault," I choke out in between sobbing gasps. "Just let me admit that for once in my fucking life—"

"*Your* fault?" He cocks his head, his back to me. "You're the one who left your journal on Elaine's vanity, where she would see it? You're the one who laughed in her face when she came to you, crying about the disgusting things she read inside it? You're the one she lunged at before she fell?"

He stands there, letting the silence say what I can't. "I didn't think so."

"Jame—"

"*Wasteland*," he says cutting me off as footsteps hurry in our direction. "You asked me about the ending once, but I gave you the wrong answer. The woman didn't fake her death because she wanted to disappear. She was ashamed. Everything she ever thought about love, and honor, and decency was turned on its head and she couldn't fucking face it. So she ran. She ran away rather than turn to the people she wasn't supposed to love or need. She was trying to be selfless—but she was fucking selfish."

He enters the hall, nearly running over Caroline. Like a storm cloud, he rolls through the house and barges from the front door.

And I know. I just do.

He's not coming back.

TWENTY-EIGHT

Night falls, but James doesn't come home. Worried, his sisters call the police, and then they find something stuck to the kitchen fridge that makes them scream and race hurriedly from the house.

Thorny left a note. That fact swirls around in hushed whispers. He left a note. A note.

A note.

They never let me see what it says. Not Marcia, Lily, or Caroline, who combine their beautiful, blond faces in sorrow. Not the police.

I'm never given a reason why.

But they don't know Thorny's secret. I slip away when no one's looking and race down to the beach. The water laughs at me, clawing its way up the shore. There's no sign of him floating. No sign of him playing in the waves with a barely legal blond.

Just silence, and…

A flash of white catches my attention, but I have to dig through the sand to free the source of it: a man's dress shirt wrapped tightly around a square object. I unfurl it slowly with numb fingers as the water laps at my sandals and the wind stings my face.

I blink several times before I fully recognize it: my copy of *Wasteland* dusted with sand. Someone taped it back together and scribbled over the final line.

You don't need me.

You never have.

But, even if you hate me now, I can try to let you go.

So hate me. Scream it out. Write the most fucked-up story you can. Let me have it.

I deserve it.

And you deserve to be heard.

I'm not supposed to be sad. The moment I so much as sigh, Caroline has my therapist on speed dial and threatens to drag me to the nearest ER.

So I can't be sad.

I can't speak, either. Everyone prods and demands I express my emotions but then tunes me out if I open my mouth. I'm just a kid. What do I know?

Nothing.

All I can do is lurk in his office with the door shut and muddle through the last bit of work Jane assigned to me. Eventually, I lose focus and wind up mouthing his message to myself over and over again.

I deserve to be heard.

But how?

His sisters sniff and sulk around Thornfield, trying desperately to compile arrangements in hushed, serious voices. They can barely look at me, let alone listen. It's when Marcia has the nerve to ask me if I have a black dress that I finally snap.

I start laughing.

"Maryanne?" She watches on in horror as I curl up in Thorny's leather armchair and snort all over his fancy desktop.

The police have already called their search off. It's only been three damn days.

But everyone is so certain.

He finally did it.

He's really gone.

But they're *wrong*. And that's the part that hurts the most as my giggles trail off and I rest my chin against my knees. They're wrong, wrong, wrong.

Thorny didn't drown. He's free, channeling the longing he expressed through every character and warped plotline for so many years. I can't be the only one in the whole damn world who sees it: He finally said, *Fuck it. Screw everyone else.*

James Thorne finally stopped wishing for the ocean and confronted James Thorne.

All it took was leaving me behind for him to be brave enough to do it.

"Maryanne?" Marcia's gone. Lily is the one creeping through the doorway now, her eyes bloodshot. She gently places something on the desk and scurries out a second later. "That came for you," she explains from the hall.

I look up, finding an envelope with the name of Thorny's old college stamped on one side. My stomach churns and I can't help releasing another high-pitched laugh that quickly fades into a sigh. He planned his disappearance perfectly, old Thorny. At least he's not here to see me fail.

It stings less if I pretend like it's a joke. I'll rip this letter open, find a rejection, and Thorny will jump from the closet. *Tada!* He got me. I don't have talent after all.

Numb with acceptance, I flick the end of the flap with my thumb and drag out the slip of paper tucked inside. For dramatic effect, I read it out loud.

"Congratulations, Ms. Mayweather," I recite, my voice breaking. "We are p-pleased to inform you…"

Of your acceptance.

With my mouth hanging open, I read that sentence over and over until I can't see anything. My eyes are blurring. The room feels too hot and stuffy. I'm suffocating. I have to take the letter out of the house and down to the beach just to get some fresh air. With the water licking at my toes, I keep reading.

We are pleased to inform you of your acceptance into the James Thorne Writer's Program at our esteemed university. Due to the caliber of your entrance exam, you have been selected as one of a handful of applicants to pen a personal essay to be published in a local newspaper at the beginning of the semester.

I frown at that. Without realizing it, I find myself wandering back into the house and sitting behind Thorny's desk. I hunt for a pen and start writing on the back of the only paper I have within reach: my acceptance letter.

I hate James Thorne, I scribble in bold, block letters. I even underline them in heavy, dark strokes.

I hate him. Maybe he wanted me to all along. Nothing inspires like heartbreak. It hurts, and it hurts, and it hurts...

But at least you know you're alive. You can scream. And kick, and shout so the whole fucking world knows you're hurting. You're in pain.

All you want is someone to see as much.

But screams fade. Bruises heal.

Nothing lasts like words. You can scribble them onto someone's soul and make them feel important. Even for a little while. You can tattoo your understanding on their heart—and even when you leave. When you're gone. When you turn away...

They always have a piece of you, hidden deep down.

Nothing heals like empty words.

Nothing soothes like little lies.

welve months later…

Life in a dorm isn't half as dramatic as the sitcoms on TV make it seem. Not even when you're the girl with the crazy, famous uncle who offed his wife and drowned in the ocean. The only downside is the fact that your mail gets left in the hallway, for anyone to find.

There's no return address on the brown package. Just a sticker for a publishing company. Inside it is a glossy novel with a cherry-red cover. I start to throw it away—I bet someone sent it as a joke. The title sure sounds like one: *A Million Crossed Lines*.

It's only when the light plays off the cover that something makes me stop. A memory, I think, of a fancy sports car in the same brilliant shade.

My heart constricts even before I flip the book open. I jump as something surprisingly heavy falls from the pages and hits the floor. Shiny. Metal. A key? Frowning, I stoop for it while brushing my eyes along the book's opening line.

"You're a liar," he told me. "No one will believe it, even if I cross the line. You're a liar."

My words.

It's *my* story, cleverly woven into a simple plot by someone more gifted at storytelling than I could ever hope to be. Once upon a time, there was a man who loved someone he wasn't supposed to. Even if it was wrong. Even if it made them both cross a million glaring red lines.

Even if it doomed them both in the end.

I'm numb when I finally finish and frantically turn to the very front page. Unsurprisingly, the author—while anonymous—penned a dedication consisting of two simple lines.

To the girl with the golden curls: I'm sorry.

To the woman with the sun-kissed hair: If you can forgive me, come find me.

Hey there!

Thank you so much for reading! If you enjoyed the story, please leave a review and recommend the book to any friend you think would love this twisted world. You'd have my eternal gratitude. Even a short sentence goes a long way!

Then, come join the rest of us dark romance lovers in my Facebook Group where you can get snippets, sneak peeks of upcoming books and even help vote on aspects of future novels.

Come to the dark side:
https://www.facebook.com/groups/lanasbeautifulmonsters/

WANT MORE STUFF TO READ?
Join my newsletter and get a **free book**! Plus, you get to stay updated with any new releases, random giveaways and exclusive sneak peeks!
https://www.lanaskybooks.com/newsletter

Other Novels: https://lanaskybooks.com/

Lana Sky is a reclusive writer in the United States who spends most of her time daydreaming about complex male characters and parenting her Cockapoo Joey. She writes dark, twisted romance across several genres. Her titles include everything from mafia romance to vampires.

facebook.com/AuthorLanaSky

twitter.com/lanasky101

amazon.com/author/lanasky

pinterest.com/lanasky101

goodreads.com/lanasky

instagram.com/lanasky101

bookbub.com/authors/lana-sky

For more titles by Lana Sky, please visit:

https://www.lanaskybooks.com

www.ingramcontent.com/pod-product-compliance
Lightning Source LLC
Chambersburg PA
CBHW070755190726
48292CB00002B/533